ASK THE EXPERTS
VOLUME ONE

ASK THE EXPERTS

VOLUME ONE

LIFE LESSONS from the MASTERS

RUDY NASH

RUPA

Published by
Rupa Publications India Pvt. Ltd 2020
7/16, Ansari Road, Daryaganj
New Delhi 110002

Sales centres:
Bengaluru Chennai
Hyderabad Jaipur Kathmandu
Kolkata Mumbai Prayagraj

P-ISBN: 978-93-89967-87-6
E-ISBN: 978-93-89967-88-3

Tenth impression 2025

14 13 12 11 10

Printed in India

Contents

Introduction

Many are the sayings of the wise,
In ancient and in modern books enrolled.

—JOHN MILTON

An ancient piece of wisdom, attributed to nearly every leading philosopher, psychologist and popular culture icon, is "when life gives you a lemon, make lemonade." Sounds refreshing and peppy, but then, how can one actually make possibilities out of a situation? Is there a science to our behavior that can actually convert problems into opportunities? Do we seek an alchemist who can take us through this motivational transformation? The answer is yes. There have always existed such alchemists who, over a period of time, have exercised their manifestos of success with aplomb. These are the thinkers who have taken their ideas from the domain of the intellectual landscape and planted them in the fertile land of human endeavor and limitless possibilities.

Self-help literature, as a phenomenon, has evolved in

phases. The first identifiable entry can be traced to the industrial revolution, which was marked by human efforts and machines, in the nineteenth century. The gradual success of the industrial age resulted in a culture of leisure and ease, especially after the Second World War. The excessive materialism and the attention seeking market of the twentieth century gave rise to a culture of 'seeking'—seeking meditation, spirituality, calmness and peace of mind. This phase was majorly influenced by eastern philosophy and life habits, trying to assuage our anxieties and fears through the balms of esoteric philosophy and individual sacrifices. And just as the world was making itself aware of the excesses of greed and cut throat competition, there came an invisible enemy—the novel corona virus, suppressing human labor, destroying industry and making the man made economy succumb.

Uncertainty looms large and anxiety creeps in from every possible human action. In these hours of crisis, we need sermons that have been time-tested and proven. Practical advice from thinkers who have been masters of the mind, who have successfully developed the concepts of self-mastery and self-knowledge, and whose teachings have become hallmarks and standards to gauge our actions in times of bewilderment and precariousness. Our anxious times of today need these everlasting sermons more than ever.

So what are we offering you in this book? In these situations and circumstances that you find yourself in today, don't you sometimes wonder what Dale Carnegie would have advised you to do? What would James Allen have told you about 'how to fix that problem'? Or for that matter, how would Emerson, Smiles, Thoreau and so many other masters, have guided you through your unsettled state of mind? That is what this book offers—life lessons from masters. By taking the questions that bother us, we have juxtaposed them with answers from each of these thinkers by culling out extracts from their time-agnostic classics on the human mind, fulfillment and achievement.

Opponents of this success maxim often object to the fact that too much notice is taken of men who have succeeded in life by helping themselves, and too little of the multitude of men who have failed. "Why should not failure," it has been asked, "have its Plutarch as well as success?" There is, indeed, no reason why failure should not have its Plutarch, except that a record of mere failure would probably be found excessively depressing as well as uninstructive reading. It is, however, shown in the following pages that failure is the best motivator for the true worker, by stimulating him to renewed efforts, evoking his best powers, and carrying him onward in terms of self-control and growth of knowledge and wisdom. Viewed in this light, failure, conquered by perseverance, is always full of interest and instruction, and this book endeavors tho show this with many examples.

The object of the book, briefly, is to re-inculcate these old-fashioned but wholesome lessons—which perhaps cannot be too often reiterated: that one must work in order to enjoy; that nothing creditable can be accomplished without application and diligence; that one must not be daunted by difficulties, but conquer them by patience and perseverance; and that, above all, one must seek elevation of character, without which capacity is worthless and worldly success amounts to naught.

Finally, the book is not one to be read and then cast aside. It is to be kept as a constant companion and an unfailing recourse in times of weariness or gloom. Human companions are not always in the mood to cheer us, and may talk about themes we dislike. But this book will converse or be silent as and when you need it to be; it will never be out of sorts or discouraged; and far from being wed to some single topic, it will speak to us at any time on any subject we desire.

ONE

How to Be Mr. Popular and Ms. Admired in Life and Office

Dale Carnegie answers from *How to Win Friends and Influence People*

Famed author and lecturer Dale Carnegie was born as Dale Carnagey (1888-1955) in Maryville, Missouri.

As a boy, Carnegie was unskilled in athletics, but learned that he could still make friends and earn respect because he had a way with words.

In 1936, after years of intense research that included reading hundreds of biographies to learn how the world's greatest leaders achieved their success, Carnegie published just such a book: How to Win Friends and Influence People. *Despite its modest initial print run of 5,000 copies, the book became a mammoth best-seller. Carnegie's book, like his classes, struck a chord with a population hungry for self-improvement, selling nearly 5 million copies during his lifetime, while being translated into every major language.*

⌣

It starts with a drop of honey…

It is an old and true maxim that 'a drop of honey catches more flies than a gallon of gall.' So with men, if you would win a man to your cause, first convince him that you are his sincere friend. Therein is a drop of honey that catches his heart; which, say what you will, is the great high road to his reason.

Daniel Webster, who looked like a god and talked like Jehovah, was one of the most successful advocates who ever pleaded a case; yet he ushered in his most powerful arguments with such friendly remarks as: it will be for the jury to consider, "This may, perhaps, be worth thinking of," "here are some facts that I trust you will not lose sight of," or "you, with your knowledge of human nature, will easily see the significance of these facts." No bulldozing. No high-pressure methods. No attempt to force his opinions on others. Webster used the soft-spoken, quiet, friendly approach, and it helped to make him famous.

Years ago, when I was a barefoot boy walking through

the woods to a country school out in Northwest Missouri, I read a fable about the sun and the wind. They quarrelled about which was the stronger, and the wind said, "I'll prove I am. See the old man down there with a coat? I bet I can get his coat off him quicker than you can."

So the sun went behind a cloud, and the wind blew until it was almost a tornado, but the harder it blew, the tighter the old man clutched his coat to him.

Finally, the wind calmed down and gave up, and then the sun came out from behind the clouds and smiled kindly on the old man. Presently, he mopped his brow and pulled off his coat. The sun then told the wind that gentleness and friendliness were always stronger than fury and force.

The use of gentleness and friendliness is demonstrated day after day by people who have learnt that a drop of honey catches more flies than a gallon of gall. Aesop was a Greek slave who lived at the court of Croesus and spun immortal fables 600 years before Christ. Yet the truths he taught about human nature are just as true in Boston and Birmingham now as they were 26 centuries ago in Athens. The sun can make you take off your coat more quickly than the wind; and kindliness, the friendly approach and appreciation can make people change their minds more readily than all the bluster and storming in the world.

BEGIN IN A FRIENDLY WAY

In talking with people, don't begin by discussing the things on which you differ. Begin by emphasizing—and keep on emphasizing—the things on which you agree. Keep emphasizing, if possible, that you are both striving for the same end and that your only difference is one of method and not of purpose.

Get the other person saying "Yes, yes" at the outset. Keep your opponent, if possible, from saying "No".

The skilful speaker gets, at the outset, a number of "Yes" responses. This sets the psychological process of the listeners moving in the affirmative direction. It is like the movement of a billiard ball. Propel in one direction, and it takes some force to deflect it; far more force to send it back in the opposite direction.

It is a very simple technique—this yes response. And yet, how much it is neglected! It often seems as if people get a sense of their own importance by antagonising others at the outset.

Get a student to say "no" at the beginning, or a customer, child, husband or wife, and it takes the wisdom and the patience of angels to transform that bristling negative into an affirmative.

Eddie Snow, who sponsors our courses in Oakland, California, tells how he became a good customer of a shop because the proprietor got him to say "yes, yes". Eddie had become interested in bow hunting and had spent considerable money in purchasing equipment and supplies from a local bow store. When his brother was visiting him he wanted to rent a bow for him from this store. The sales clerk told him they didn't rent bows, so Eddie phoned another bow store. Eddie described what happened:

"A very pleasant gentleman answered the phone. His response to my question for a rental was completely different from the other place. He said he was sorry but they no longer rented bows because they couldn't afford to do so. He then asked me if I had rented before. I replied, 'Yes, several years ago.' He reminded me that I probably paid $25 to $30 for the rental. I said 'yes' again. He then asked if I was the kind of person who liked to save money. Naturally, I answered 'yes.' He went on to explain that they had bow sets with all the necessary equipment on sale for $34.95. I could buy a complete set for only $4.95 more than I could rent one. He explained that is why they had discontinued renting them. Did I think that was reasonable? My 'yes' response led to a purchase of the set, and when I picked it up I purchased several more items at this shop and have since become a regular customer."

THE MAGIC FORMULA

Remember that other people may be totally wrong. But they don't think so. Don't condemn them. Any fool can do that. Try to understand them. Only wise, tolerant, exceptional people even try to do that.

There is a reason why the other man thinks and acts as he does. Ferret out that reason—and you have the key to his actions, perhaps to his personality.

Try honestly to put yourself in his place.

If you say to yourself, "How would I feel, how would I react if I were in his shoes?" you will save yourself time and irritation, for "by becoming interested in the cause, we are less likely to dislike the effect." And, in addition, you will sharply increase your skill in human relationships.

Sam Douglas of Hempstead, New York, used to tell his wife that she spent too much time working on their lawn, pulling weeds, fertilising, cutting the grass twice a week when the lawn didn't look any hetter than it had when they moved into their home four years earlier. Naturally, she was distressed by his remarks, and each time he made such remarks the balance of the evening was ruined.

After taking our course, Mr Douglas realised how foolish he had been all those years. It never occurred to him that she enjoyed doing that work and she might really appreciate a compliment on her diligence.

One evening after dinner, his wife said she wanted to pull some weeds and invited him to keep her company. He first declined, but then thought better of it and went out after her and began to help her pull weeds. She was visibly pleased, and together they spent an hour in hard work and pleasant conversation.

After that he often helped her with the gardening and complimented her on how fine the lawn looked, what a fantastic job she was doing with a yard where the soil was like concrete. Result: a happier life for both because he had learnt to look at things from her point of view—even if the subject was only weeds.

Tomorrow, before asking anyone to buy your product or contribute to your favourite charity, why not pause and close your eyes and try to think the whole thing through from another person's point of view? Ask yourself: "Why should he or she want to do it?" True, this will take time, but it will avoid making enemies and will get better results—and with less friction and less shoe leather.

"I would rather walk the sidewalk in front of a person's office for two hours before an interview," said Dean Donham of the Harvard business school, "than step into that office without a perfectly clear idea of what I was going to say and what that person—from my knowledge of his or her interests and motives—was likely to answer."

It is enormously important to think always in terms of

the other person's point of view, and see things from that person's angle, as well as your own.

AN APPEAL THAT EVERYBODY LIKES

l was reared on the edge of the Jesse James country out in Missouri, and I visited the James farm at Kearney, Missouri, where the son of Jesse James was then living. His wife told me stories of how Jesse robbed trains and held up banks and then gave money to the neighbouring farmers to pay off their mortgages.

Jesse James probably regarded himself as an idealist at heart, just as Dutch Schultz, 'Two Gun' Crowley, Al Capone and many other organised crime 'godfathers' did generations later. The fact is that all people you meet have a high regard for themselves and like to be fine and unselfish in their own estimation.

J. Pierpont Morgan observed, in one of his analytical interludes, that a person usually has two reasons for doing a thing: one that sounds good and a real one.

The person himself will think of the real reason. You don't need to emphasise that. But all of us, being idealists at heart, like to think of motives that sound good. So, in order to change people, appeal to the nobler motives.

Is that too idealistic to work in business? Let's see. Let's take the case of Hamilton J. Farrell of the Farrell-Mitchell

Company of Glenolden, Pennsylvania. Mr Farrell had a disgruntled tenant who threatened to move. The tenant's lease still had four months to run; nevertheless, he served notice that he was vacating immediately, regardless of lease.

"These people had lived in my house all winter—the most expensive part of the year," Mr Farrell said as he told the story to the class, "and I knew it would be difficult to rent the apartment again before fall. I could see all that rent income going over the hill and believe me, I saw red.

"Now, ordinarily, I would have waded into that tenant and advised him to read his lease again. I would have pointed out that if he moved, the full balance of his rent would fall due at once—and that I could, and would move to collect.

"However, instead of flying off the handle and making a scene, I decided to try other tactics. So I started like this: 'Mr Doe,' I said, 'I have listened to your story, and I still don't believe you intend to move. Years in the renting business have taught me something about human nature, and I sized you up in the first place as being a man of your word. In fact, I'm so sure of it that I'm willing to take a gamble.

"'Now, here's my proposition. Lay your decision on the table for a few days and think it over. If you come back to me between now and the first of the month, when your rent is due, and tell me you still intend to move, I give you my word I will accept your decision as final. I will privilege you to move and admit to myself I've been wrong in my judgement. But I still believe you're a man of your word and will live up to your contract. For after all, we are either men or monkeys—and the choice usually lies with ourselves!'

"Well, when the new month came around, this gentleman came to see me and paid his rent in person. He and his wife had talked it over he said—and decided to stay. They had concluded that the only honourable thing to do was to live up to their lease."

When Cyrus H.K. Curtis, the poor boy from Maine, was starting on his meteoric career, which was destined to make him millions as owner of The Saturday Evening Post and the Ladies' Home Journal, he couldn't afford to pay his contributors the prices that other magazines paid. He couldn't afford to hire first-class authors to write for money alone. So he appealed to their nobler motives. For example, he persuaded even Louisa May Alcott, the immortal author of Little Women, to write for him when she was at the flood tide of her fame; and he did it by offering to send a cheque for a hundred dollars, not to her, but to her favourite charity.

Right here the sceptic may say: "Oh, that stuff is all right for Farell and Curtis or a sentimental novelist. But, I'd like to see you make it work with the tough babies I have to collect bills form!"

You may be right. Nothing will work in all cases—and nothing will work with all people. If you are satisfied with the results you are now getting, why change? If you are not satisfied, why not experiment?

DO THIS AND YOU'LL BE WELCOME ANYWHERE

Why read this book to find out how to win friends? Why not study the technique of the greatest winner of friends the world has ever known? Who is he? You may meet him tomorrow coming down the street. When you get within ten feet of him, he will begin to wag his tail. If you stop and pat him he will almost jump out of his skin to show you how much he likes you. And you know that behind this show of affection on his part, there are no ulterior motives: he doesn't want to sell you any real estate, and he doesn't want to marry you.

Did you ever stop to think that a dog is the only animal that doesn't have to work for a living? A hen has to lay eggs, a cow has to give milk and a canary has to sing. But a dog makes his living by giving you nothing but love.

When I was five years old, my father bought a little yellow-haired pup for fifty cents. He was the light and joy of my childhood. Every afternoon about four-thirty, he would sit in the front yard with his beautiful eyes staring steadfastly at the path, and as soon as he heard my voice or saw me swinging my dinner pail through the buck brush, he was off like a shot, racing breathlessly up the hill to greet me with leaps of joy and barks of sheer ecstasy.

Tippy was my constant companion for five years. Then one tragic night—I shall never forget it—he was killed within ten feet of my head, killed by lightning. Tippy's death was the tragedy of my boyhood.

You never read a book on psychology, Tippy. You didn't need to. You knew by some divine instinct that you can make more friends in two months by becoming genuinely interested in other people than you can in two years by trying to get other people interested in you. Let me repeat that. You can make more friends in two months by becoming interested in other people than you can in two years by trying to get other people interested in you.

Yet I know and you know people who blunder through life trying to wigwag other people into becoming interested in them.

Of course, it doesn't work. People are not interested in you. They are not interested in me. They are interested in themselves—morning, noon and after dinner.

The New York Telephone Company made a detailed study of telephone conversations to find out which word is the most frequently used. You have guessed it: it is the personal pronoun 'I.' 'I.' 'I.' It was used 3,900 times in 500 telephone conversations. 'I.' 'I.' 'I.' 'I.'

When you see a group photograph that you are in, whose picture do you look for first?

If we merely try to impress people and get people interested in us, we will never have many true, sincere friends. Friends, real friends, are not made that way.

That, too, was one of the secrets of Theodore Roosevelt's astonishing popularity. Even his servants loved him. His valet, James E. Amos, wrote a book about him entitled Theodore Roosevelt, Hero to His Valet. In that book Amos relates this illuminating incident:

My wife one time asked the President about a bobwhite. She had never seen one and he described it to her fully. Sometime later, the telephone at our cottage rang. [Amos and his wife lived in a little cottage on the Roosevelt estate at Oyster Bay.] My wife answered it and it was Mr Roosevelt himself. He had called her, he said, to tell her that there was a bobwhite outside her window and that if she would look out she might see it. Little things like that were so characteristic of him. Whenever he went by our cottage even though we were out of sight, we would hear him call out: "Oo-oo-oo, Annie?" or "Oo-oo-oo, James!" It was just a friendly greeting as he went by.

How could employees keep from liking a man like that? How could anyone keep from liking him?

Roosevelt called at the White House one day when the President and Mrs Taft were away. His honest liking for humble people was shown by the fact that he greeted all the old White House servants by name, even the scullery maids.

"But when he saw Alice, the kitchen maid," writes Archie Butt, "he asked her if she still made corn bread. Alice told him that she sometimes made it for the servants, but no one ate it upstairs.

"'They show bad taste,' Roosevelt boomed, 'and I'll tell the President so when I see him.'

"Alice brought a piece to him on a plate, and he went over to the office eating it as he went and greeting gardeners and labourers as he passed...

"He addressed each person just as he had addressed them in the past. Ike Hoover, who had been head usher at the White House for forty years, said with tears in his eyes: 'It is the only happy day we had in nearly two years, and not one of us would exchange it for a hundred-dollar bill.'"

All of us, be we workers in a factory, clerks in an office or even a king upon his throne—all of us like people who admire us. Take the German Kaiser, for example. At the close of World War I he was probably the most savagely and universally despised man on this earth. Even his own nation turned against him when he fled over into Holland to save his neck. The hatred against him was so intense that millions of people would have loved to tear him limb from limb or burn him at the stake. In the midst of all this forest fire of fury, one little boy wrote the Kaiser a simple, sincere letter glowing with kindliness and admiration. This little boy said that no matter what the others thought, he would always love Wilhelm as his Emperor. The Kaiser was deeply touched by this letter and invited the little boy to come to see him. The boy came, so did his mother—and the Kaiser married her. That little boy didn't need to read a book on how to win friends and influence people. He knew how instinctively.

If we want to make friends, let's put ourselves out to do things for other people—things that require time, energy, unselfishness and thoughtfulness. When the Duke of Windsor was Prince of Wales, he was scheduled to tour South America, and before he started out on that tour he spent months studying Spanish so that he could make public talks in the language of the country; and the South Americans loved him for it.

For years I made it a point to find out the birthdays of my friends. How? Although I haven't the foggiest bit of faith in astrology, I began by asking the other party whether he believed the date of one's birth has anything to do with character and disposition. I then asked him or her to tell me the month and day of birth. If he or she said 24 November, for example, I kept repeating to myself, "24 November, 24 November." The minute my friend's back was turned I wrote down the name and birthday and later would transfer it to a birthday book. At the beginning of each year, I had these birthday dates scheduled in my calendar pad so that they came to my attention automatically. When the natal day arrived, there was my letter or telegram. What a hit it made! I was frequently the only person on earth who remembered.

If we want to make friends, let's greet people with animation and enthusiasm. When somebody calls you on the telephone use the same psychology. Say 'Hello' in tones that bespeak how pleased you are to have the person call. Many companies train their telephone operators to greet all callers in a tone of voice that radiates interest and enthusiasm. The caller feels the company is concerned about them. Let's remember that when we answer the telephone tomorrow.

Showing a genuine interest in others not only wins friends for you, but may develop in its customers a loyalty to your company.

A show of interest, as with every other principle of human relations, must be sincere. It must pay off not only for the person showing the interest, but for the person receiving the attention. It is a two-way street—both parties benefit.

If you want others to like you, if you want to develop real friendships, if you want to help others at the same time as you help yourself, keep this principle in mind:

- Try honestly to see things from the other person's point of view.
- For better or worse, you must play your own instrument in the orchestra of life.
- When you are wrong, admit it to yourself.
- A man convinced against his will is of the same opinion still.
- Be sympathetic to the other person's ideas and desires.

TWO

How to Change Your Life by Changing Your Thoughts

James Allen answers from *As the Man Thinketh*

*In the words of James Allen (1864-1912) himself, this essay
(the result of meditation and experience) is not intended as
an exhaustive treatise on the much-written-upon subject of
the power of thought. It is suggestive rather than explanatory,
its object being to stimulate men and women to the discovery
and perception of the truth that—"They are themselves
makers of themselves."*

> *Mind is the Master power that moulds and makes,*
> *And Man is Mind, and evermore he takes*
> *The tool of Thought, and, shaping what he wills,*
> *Brings forth a thousand joys, a thousand ills,*

He thinks in secret, and it comes to pass,
Environment is but his looking-glass.

The aphorism, "As a man thinketh in his heart so is he," not only embraces the whole of a man's being, but is so comprehensive as to reach out to every condition and circumstance of his life. A man is literally what he thinks, his character being the complete sum of all his thoughts.

As the plant springs from, and could not be without, the seed, so every act of a man springs from the hidden seeds of thought, and could not have appeared without them. This applies equally to those acts called "spontaneous" and "unpremeditated" as to those, which are deliberately executed.

Act is the blossom of thought, and joy and suffering are its fruits; thus does a man garner in the sweet and bitter fruitage of his own husbandry.

Man is made or unmade by himself; in the armoury of thought he forges the weapons by which he destroys himself; he also fashions the tools with which he builds for himself heavenly mansions of joy and strength and peace.

By the right choice and true application of thought, man ascends to the Divine Perfection; by the abuse and wrong application of thought, he descends below the level of the beast. Between these two extremes are all the grades of character, and man is their maker and master.

Of all the beautiful truths pertaining to the soul which have been restored and brought to light in this age, none is more gladdening or fruitful of divine promise and confidence than this—that man is the master of thought, the molder of character, and the maker and shaper of condition, environment, and destiny. As a being of Power, Intelligence, and Love, and the lord of his own thoughts, man holds the key to every situation, and contains within himself that transforming and regenerative agency by which he may make himself what he wills.

Man is always the master, even in his weaker and most abandoned state; but in his weakness and degradation he is the foolish master who misgoverns his "household." When he begins to reflect upon his condition, and to search diligently for the Law upon which his being is established, he then becomes the wise master, directing his energies with intelligence, and fashioning his thoughts to fruitful issues. Such is the conscious master, and man can only thus become by discovering within himself the laws of thought; which discovery is totally a matter of application, self-analysis, and experience.

EFFECT OF THOUGHT ON CIRCUMSTANCES

Man's mind may be likened to a garden, which may be intelligently cultivated or allowed to run wild; but whether cultivated or neglected, it must, and will, bring forth. If no useful seeds are put into it, then an abundance of useless weed-seeds will fall therein, and will continue to produce their kind.

Just as a gardener cultivates his plot, keeping it free from weeds, and growing the flowers and fruits which he requires, so may a man tend the garden of his mind, weeding out all the wrong, useless, and impure thoughts, and cultivating toward perfection the flowers and fruits of right, useful, and pure thoughts. By pursuing this process, a man sooner or later discovers that he is the master-gardener of his soul, the director of his life. He also reveals, within himself, the laws of thought, and understands, with ever-increasing accuracy, how the thought-forces and mind elements operate in the shaping of his character, circumstances, and destiny. Thought and character are one, and as character can only manifest and discover itself through environment and circumstance, the outer conditions of a person's life will always be found to be harmoniously related to his inner state. This does not mean that a man's circumstances at any given time are an indication of his entire character, but that those circumstances are so intimately connected with some vital thought-element within himself that, for the time being, they are indispensable to his development.

Every man is where he is by the law of his being; the thoughts which he has built into his character have brought him there, and in the arrangement of his life there is no element of chance, but all is the result of a law which cannot err. This is just as true of those who feel "out of harmony" with their surroundings as of those who are contented with them.

Man is buffeted by circumstances so long as he believes himself to be the creature of outside conditions, but when he realizes that he is a creative power, and that he may command the hidden soil and seeds of his being out of which circumstances grow, he then becomes the rightful master of himself.

That circumstances grow out of thought every man knows who has for any length of time practiced self-control and self-purification, for he will have noticed that the alteration in his circumstances has been in exact ratio with his altered mental condition. So true is this that when a man earnestly applies himself to remedy the defects in his character, and makes swift and marked progress, he passes rapidly through a succession of vicissitudes.

The soul attracts that which it secretly harbours; that which it loves, and also that which it fears; it reaches the height of its cherished aspirations; it falls to the level of its unchastened desires,—and circumstances are the means by which the soul receives its own.

Every thought-seed sown or allowed to fall into the mind, and to take root there, produces its own, blossoming sooner or later into act, and bearing its own fruitage of opportunity and circumstance. Good thoughts bear good fruit, bad thoughts bad fruit. The outer world of circumstance shapes itself to the inner world of thought, and both pleasant and unpleasant external conditions are factors, which make for the ultimate good of the individual. As the reaper of his own harvest, man learns both by suffering and bliss.

Men do not attract that which they want, but that which they are. Their whims, fancies, and ambitions are thwarted at every step, but their inmost thoughts and desires are fed with their own food, be it foul or clean. The "divinity that shapes our ends" is in ourselves; it is our very self. Only himself manacles man: thought and action are the gaolers of Fate—they imprison, being base; they are also the angels of Freedom—they liberate, being noble. Not what he wishes and prays for does a man get, but what he justly earns. His wishes and prayers are only gratified and answered when they harmonize with his thoughts and actions.

In the light of this truth, what, then, is the meaning of "fighting against circumstances?" It means that a man is continually revolting against an effect without, while all the time he is nourishing and preserving its cause in his heart. That cause may take the form of a conscious vice or an unconscious weakness; but whatever it is, it stubbornly retards the efforts of its possessor, and thus calls aloud for remedy.

Men are anxious to improve their circumstances, but are unwilling to improve themselves; they therefore remain bound. The man who does not shrink from self-crucifixion can never fail to accomplish the object upon which his heart is set. This is as true of earthly as of heavenly things. Even the man whose sole object is to acquire wealth must be prepared to make great personal sacrifices before he can accomplish his object; and how much more so he who would realize a strong and well-poised life?

Here is a man who is wretchedly poor. He is extremely anxious that his surroundings and home comforts should be improved, yet all the time he shirks his work, and considers he is justified in trying to deceive his employer on the ground of the insufficiency of his wages. Such a man does not understand the simplest rudiments of those principles which are the basis of true prosperity, and is not only totally unfitted to rise out of his wretchedness, but is actually attracting to himself a still deeper wretchedness by dwelling in, and acting out, indolent, deceptive, and unmanly thoughts.

Here is a rich man who is the victim of a painful and

persistent disease as the result of gluttony. He is willing to give large sums of money to get rid of it, but he will not sacrifice his gluttonous desires. He wants to gratify his taste for rich and unnatural viands and have his health as well. Such a man is totally unfit to have health, because he has not yet learned the first principles of a healthy life.

Here is an employer of labour who adopts crooked measures to avoid paying the regulation wage, and, in the hope of making larger profits, reduces the wages of his workpeople. Such a man is altogether unfitted for prosperity, and when he finds himself bankrupt, both as regards reputation and riches, he blames circumstances, not knowing that he is the sole author of his condition.

Circumstances, however, are so complicated, thought is so deeply rooted, and the conditions of happiness vary so, vastly with individuals, that a man's entire soul-condition (although it may be known to himself) cannot be judged by another from the external aspect of his life alone. A man may be honest in certain directions, yet suffer privations; a man may be dishonest in certain directions, yet acquire wealth; but the conclusion usually formed that the one man fails because of his particular honesty, and that the other prospers because of his particular dishonesty, is the result of a superficial judgment, which assumes that the dishonest man is almost totally corrupt, and the honest man almost entirely virtuous. In the light of a deeper knowledge and wider experience such judgment is found to be erroneous. The dishonest man may have some admirable virtues, which the other does, not possess; and the honest man obnoxious vices which are absent in the other. The honest man reaps the good results of his honest thoughts and acts; he also brings upon himself the sufferings, which his vices produce. The dishonest man likewise garners his own suffering and happiness. It is pleasing to human vanity to believe that one suffers because of one's virtue; but not until a man has extirpated every sickly, bitter, and impure thought from his mind, and washed every sinful stain from his soul, can he be in a position to know and declare that his sufferings are the result of his good, and not of his bad qualities; and on the way to, yet long before he has reached, that supreme perfection, he will have found, working in his mind and life, the Great Law which is absolutely just, and which cannot, therefore, give good for evil, evil for good. Possessed of such knowledge, he will then know, looking back upon his past ignorance and blindness, that his life is, and always was, justly ordered, and that all his past experiences, good and bad, were the equitable outworking of his evolving, yet unevolved self.

Good thoughts and actions can never produce bad results; bad thoughts and actions can never produce good results. This is but saying that nothing can come from corn but corn, nothing from nettles but nettles. Men understand this law in the natural world, and work with it; but few understand it in the mental and moral world (though its operation there is just as simple and undeviating), and they, therefore, do not co-operate with it.

Suffering is always the effect of wrong thought in some direction. It is an indication that the individual is out of harmony with himself, with the Law of his being. The sole and supreme use of suffering is to purify, to burn out all that is useless and impure. Suffering ceases for him who is pure. There could be no object in burning gold after the dross had been removed, and a perfectly pure and enlightened being could not suffer.

The circumstances, which a man encounters with suffering, are the result of his own mental in harmony. The circumstances, which a man encounters with blessedness, are the result of his own mental harmony. Blessedness, not material possessions, is the measure of right thought; wretchedness, not lack of material possessions, is the measure of wrong thought. A man may be cursed and rich; he may be blessed and poor. Blessedness and riches are only joined together when the riches are rightly and wisely used; and the poor man only descends into wretchedness when he regards his lot as a burden unjustly imposed.

Indigence and indulgence are the two extremes of wretchedness. They are both equally unnatural and the result of mental disorder. A man is not rightly conditioned until he is a happy, healthy, and prosperous being; and happiness, health, and prosperity are the result of a harmonious adjustment of the inner with the outer, of the man with his surroundings.

A man only begins to be a man when he ceases to whine and revile, and commences to search for the hidden justice which regulates his life. And as he adapts his mind to that regulating factor, he ceases to accuse others as the cause of his condition, and builds himself up in strong and noble thoughts; ceases to kick against circumstances, but begins to use them as aids to his more rapid progress, and as a means of discovering the hidden powers and possibilities within himself.

Law, not confusion, is the dominating principle in the universe; justice, not injustice, is the soul and substance of life; and righteousness, not corruption, is the moulding and moving force in the spiritual government of the world. This being so, man has but to right himself to find that the universe is right; and during the process of putting himself right he will find that as he alters his thoughts towards things and other people, things and other people will alter towards him.

The proof of this truth is in every person, and it therefore admits of easy investigation by systematic introspection and self-analysis. Let a man radically alter his thoughts, and he will be astonished at the rapid transformation it will effect in the material conditions of his life. Men imagine that thought can be kept secret, but it cannot; it rapidly crystallizes into habit, and habit solidifies into circumstance. Bestial thoughts crystallize into habits of drunkenness and sensuality, which solidify into circumstances of destitution and disease: impure thoughts of every kind crystallize into enervating and confusing habits, which solidify into distracting and adverse circumstances: thoughts of fear, doubt, and indecision crystallize into weak, unmanly, and irresolute habits, which solidify into circumstances of failure, indigence, and slavish dependence: lazy thoughts crystallize into habits of uncleanliness and dishonesty, which solidify into circumstances of foulness and beggary: hateful and condemnatory thoughts crystallize into habits of accusation and violence, which solidify into circumstances of injury and persecution: selfish thoughts of all kinds crystallize into habits of self-seeking, which solidify into circumstances more or less distressing. On the other hand, beautiful thoughts of all kinds crystallize into habits of grace and kindliness, which solidify into genial and sunny circumstances: pure thoughts crystallize into habits of temperance and self-control, which solidify into circumstances of repose and peace: thoughts of courage, self-reliance, and decision crystallize into manly habits, which solidify into circumstances of success, plenty, and freedom: energetic thoughts crystallize into habits of cleanliness and industry, which solidify into circumstances of pleasantness: gentle and forgiving thoughts crystallize into habits of gentleness, which solidify into protective and preservative circumstances: loving and unselfish thoughts crystallize into habits of self-forgetfulness for others, which solidify into circumstances of sure and abiding prosperity and true riches.

A particular train of thought persisted in, be it good or bad, cannot fail to produce its results on the character and circumstances. A man cannot directly choose his circumstances, but he can choose his thoughts, and so indirectly, yet surely, shape his circumstances.

Nature helps every man to the gratification of the thoughts, which he most encourages, and opportunities are presented which will most speedily bring to the surface both the good and evil thoughts.

Let a man cease from his sinful thoughts, and all the world will soften towards him, and be ready to help him; let him put away his weakly and sickly thoughts, and lo, opportunities will spring up on every hand to aid his strong resolves; let him encourage good thoughts, and no hard fate shall bind him down to wretchedness and shame. The world is your kaleidoscope, and the varying combinations of colors, which at every succeeding moment it presents to you are the exquisitely adjusted pictures of your ever-moving thoughts.

- A man cannot directly choose his circumstances, but he can choose his thoughts.
- cease from his sinful thoughts.
- Put away your weak and sick thoughts.
- Thoughts crystallize into habits and habits in turn convert into circumstance. So, nurture happy and positive thoughts.
- As you alter your thoughts towards things and other people, things and other people will alter towards you.

THREE

How to Realize Your Potential by Taking More Risks

Orison Swett Marden answers from *The Victorious Attitude*

Orison Swett Marden (1848-1924), founder of Success Magazine, *is also considered to be the founder of the modern "success" movement in America. He certainly bridged the gap between the old, narrow notions of success and the new, more comprehensive models made popular by best-selling authors such as Napoleon Hill, Clement Stone, Dale Carnegie, Og Mandino, Earl Nightingale, Norman Vincent Peale, and today's authors Stephen R. Covey, Anthony Robbins, and Brian Tracy.*

Go boldly; go serenely, go augustly;
Who can withstand thee then!
BROWNING

What a grasp the mind would have if we could always hold the victorious attitude toward everything! Sweeping past obstacles and reaching out into the energy of the universe it would gather to itself material for building a life in its own image.

To be a conqueror in appearance, in one's bearing, is the first step toward success. It inspires confidence in others as well as in oneself.

Walk, talk and act as though you were a somebody, and you are more likely to become such. Move about among your fellowmen as though you believe you are a man of importance. Let victory speak from your face and express itself in your manner. Carry yourself like one who is conscious he has a splendid mission, a grand aim in life. Radiate a hopeful, expectant, cheerful atmosphere. In other words, be a good advertisement of the winner you are trying to be.

Doubts, fears, despondency, lack of confidence, will not only give you away in the estimation of others and brand you as a weakling, a probable failure, but they will react upon your mentality and destroy your self-confidence, your initiative, your efficiency. They are telltales, proclaiming to every one you meet that you are losing out in the game of life. A triumphant expression inspires trust, makes a favorable impression. A despondent, discouraged expression creates distrust, makes an unfavorable impression.

If you don't look cheerful and appear and act like a winner nobody will want you. Every man will turn a deaf ear to your plea for work. No matter if you are jobless and have been out of work for a long time you must keep up a winning appearance, a victorious attitude, or you will lose the very thing you are after. The world has little use for whiners, or long-faced failures.

It is difficult to get very far away from people's estimate of us. A bad first impression often creates a prejudice that it is impossible afterwards wholly to remove. Hence the importance of always radiating a cheerful, uplifting atmosphere, an atmosphere that will be a commendation instead of a condemnation. Not that we should deceive by trying to appear what we are not, but we should always keep our best side out, not our second best or our worst. Our personal appearance is our show window where we insert what we have for sale, and we are judged by what we put there.

The victorious idea of life, not its failure side, its

disappointed side; the triumphant, not the thwarted-ambition side, is the thing to keep ever uppermost in the mind, for it is this that will lead you to the light. You must give the impression that you are a success, or that you have qualities that will make you successful, that you are making good, or no recommendation or testimonial however strong will counteract the unfavorable impression you make.

So much of our progress in life depends upon our reputation, upon making a favorable impression upon others, that it is of the utmost importance to cultivate mental forcefulness. It is the mind that colors the personality, gives it its tone and character. If we cultivate will power, decision, positive instead of negative thinking, we cannot help making an impression of masterfulness, and everybody knows that this is the qualification that does things. It is masterfulness, force, that achieves results, and if we do not express it in our appearance people will not have confidence in our achieving ability. They may think that we can sell goods behind a counter, work under orders, carry out some mechanical routine with faithfulness and precision, but they will not think we are fitted for leadership, that we can command resources to meet possible crises or big emergencies.

Never say or do anything which will show the earmarks of a weakling, of a nobody, of a failure. Never permit yourself to assume a poverty-stricken attitude. Never show the world a gloomy, pessimistic face, which is an admission that life has been a disappointment to you instead of a glorious triumph. Never admit by your speech, your appearance, your gait, your manner, that there is anything wrong with you. Hold up your head. Walk erect. Look everybody in the face. No matter how poor you may be, or how shabby your clothes, whether you are jobless, homeless, friendless even, show the world that you respect yourself, that you believe in yourself, and that, no matter how hard the way, you are marching on to victory. Show by your expression that you can think and plan for yourself, that you have a forceful mentality.

The victorious, triumphant attitude will put you in command of resources which a timid, self-depreciating, failure attitude will drive from you.

This was well illustrated by a visitor to the Athenæum Library in Boston. Ignorant of the fact that members only were entitled to its special privileges, this visitor entered the place with a confident bearing, seated herself in a comfortable window seat, and spent a delightful morning reading and writing letters. In the evening she called on a friend and in the course of conversation, referred to her morning at the Athenæum.

"Why, I didn't know you were a member!" exclaimed the friend.

"A member! No," said the lady. "I am not a member.

But what difference does that make?"

The friend, who held an Athenæum card of membership, smiled and replied:

"Only this, that none but members are supposed to enjoy the privileges of which you availed yourself this morning!"

Our manner and our appearance are determined by our mental outlook. If we see only failure ahead we will act and look like failures. We have already failed. If we expect success, see it waiting for us a little bit up the road, we will act and look like successes. We have already succeeded. The failure attitude loses; the victorious attitude wins.

Had the lady in Boston had any doubt of her right to enter the Athenæum and freely to use all its conveniences, her manner would have betrayed it. The library attendants would have noticed it at once, and have asked her to show her card of membership. But her assured air gave the impression that she was a member. Her victorious attitude dominated the situation, and put her in command of resources which otherwise she could not have controlled.

The spirit in which you face your work, in which you grapple with a difficulty, the spirit in which you meet your problem, whether you approach it like a conqueror, with courage, a vigorous resolution, with firmness, or with timidity, doubt, fear, will determine whether your career will be one grand victory or a complete failure.

It is a great thing so to carry yourself wherever you go that when people see you coming they will say to themselves, "Here comes a winner! Here is a man who dominates everything he touches."

Thinking of yourself as habitually lucky will tend to make you so, just as thinking of yourself as habitually unlucky and always talking about your failures and your cruel fate will tend to make you unlucky. The attitude of mind which your thoughts and convictions produce is a real force which builds or tears down. The habit of always seeing yourself as a fortunate individual, the feeling grateful just for being alive, for being allowed to live on this beautiful earth and to have a chance to make good will put your mind in a creative, producing attitude.

We should all go through life as though we were sent here with a sublime mission to lift, to help, to boost, and not to depress and discourage, and so discredit the plan of the Creator. Our conduct should show that we are on this earth to play a magnificent part in life's drama, to make a splendid contribution to humanity.

The majority of people seem to take it for granted that life is a great gambling game in which the odds are heavily against them. This conviction colors their whole attitude, and is responsible for innumerable failures.

In the betting machines used by horse racing gamblers the bettors make the odds. If, for example, five hundred persons bet on a certain horse, and a hundred bet on another, then the first horse automatically becomes a five to one choice, and the odds in favor of his winning are five to one. In the game of life most of us start out by putting the odds on our failure.

In horse race gambling the judgment that forms the basis of belief as to the winning horse has a comparatively secure foundation in a knowledge of the qualifications of the different racers. In life gambling it is merely the unsupported opinion or viewpoint of the individual that puts the odds against himself. The majority of people look on the probability of their winning out in the life game in any distinctive way as highly improbable. When they look around and see how comparatively few of the multitudes of men and women in the world are winning they say to themselves, "Why should I think that I have a greater percentage of chance in my favor than others about me? These people have as much ability as I have, perhaps more, and if they can do no more than grub along from hand to mouth, of what use is it for me to struggle against fate?"

When people believe and figure that they cannot, and therefore never will, be successes, and conduct themselves according to their conviction: when they take their places in life not as probable winners, but as probable losers, is it any wonder that the odds are heavily against them?

"Mad! Insane! Eccentric!" we say when some miserable

recluse dies in squalor and wretchedness,—"Starved," the coroner's inquest finds, although bank books revealing large deposits, or else hoards of gold, are discovered hidden away in nooks and crannies of the wretched miser's quarters.

Are such persons, whom we call mad, insane, eccentric, who stint and save, and hoard in the midst of plenty, refusing even to buy food to keep them alive, any worse than those who face life in a poverty-stricken, failure attitude, refusing to see and enjoy the riches, the glories all around them? Is it any wonder that life is a disappointment to them? Is it any wonder that they see only what they look for, get only what they expect?

What would you think of an actor who was trying to play the part of a great hero, but who insisted on assuming the attitude of a coward, and thinking like one; who wore the expression of a man who did not believe he could do the thing he had undertaken, who felt that he was out of place, that he never was made to play the part he was attempting?

Naturally you would say the man never could succeed on the stage, and that if he ever hoped to win success, the first thing he should do would be to try to think himself the character, as well as to look the part, he was trying to portray. That is just what the great actor does. He flings himself with all his might into the rôle he is playing. He sees himself as, and feels that he is actually, the character he is impersonating. He lives the part he is playing on the stage, whether it be that of a beggar or a hero. If he is playing the part of a hero he acts like a hero, thinks and talks like a hero. His very manner radiates heroism. And vice versa, if the part he takes is that of a beggar, he dresses like one, thinks like one, bows, cringes and whines like a beggar.

Now, if you are trying to be successful you must act like a successful person, carry yourself like one, talk, act and think like a winner. You must radiate victory wherever you go. You must maintain your attitude by believing in the thing you are trying to do. If you persist in looking and acting like a failure or a very mediocre or doubtful success, if you keep telling everybody how unlucky you are, and that you do not believe you will win out because success is only for a few, that the great majority of people must be hewers of wood and drawers of water, you will be about as much of a success as the actor who attempts to personate a certain type of character while looking, thinking and acting exactly like its opposite.

By a psychological law we attract that which corresponds with our mental attitude, with our faith, our hopes, our expectations, or with our doubts and fears. If this were fully understood, and used as a working principle in life, we would have no poverty, no failures, no criminals, no down-and-outs. We would not see people everywhere with expressions which indicate that there is very little enjoyment in living; that it is a serious question with them whether life is really worth while, whether it really pays to struggle on in a miserable world where rewards are so few and uncertain and pains and penalties so numerous and so certain.

Every boy, every girl should be taught to assume the victorious attitude toward life. All through a youth's education the idea should be drilled into him that he is intended to be a winner in life, that he is himself a prince, a god in the making. From his cradle up he should be taught to hold his head high, and to look on himself as a son of the King of kings, destined for great things.

No child is properly reared and educated until he or she knows how to lead a victorious life. This is what true education means—victory over self, victory over conditions.

It always pains me to hear a youth who ought to be full of hope and high promise express a doubt as to his future career. To hear him talk about his possible failure sounds like treason to his Creator. Why, youth itself is victory. Youth is a great prophecy, the forerunner of a superb fulfillment. A young man or a young woman talking about failure is like beauty talking about ugliness; like superb health dwelling upon weakness and disease; like perfection dwelling upon imperfection. Youth means victory, because everything in the life of the healthy boy or girl is looking upward. There is no downgrade in normal youth; it is its nature to climb, to look up. Its very atmosphere should breathe hope, superb promise of the future.

If all children were reared with such a triumphant conception of life, with such an unshakable belief in their heritage from God, that nothing could discourage them, we would hear no talk of failure; we would soon sight the millenium. If they were made to understand that there is only one failure to be feared,—failure to make good, the failure of character, the failure to keep growing, to ennoble and enrich one's life, this world would be a paradise.

Just think what would happen if all of the down-and-outs to-day, all of the people who look upon themselves as failures or as dwarfs of what they ought to be, could only get this victorious, this triumphant, idea of life, if they could only once glimpse their own possibilities and assume the triumphant attitude! They would never again be satisfied to grovel. If they once got a glimpse of their divinity, once saw themselves in the sublime robes of their power, they never again would be satisfied with the rags of their poverty.

But instead of trying to improve their condition, to get away from their failure, poverty-stricken atmosphere, they cling the more closely to it and sink deeper and deeper in the quagmire of their own making.

Everywhere we find whining, miserable people

grumbling at everything, complaining that "life is not worth living," that "the game is not worth the candle," that "life is a cheat, a losing game."

Life is not a losing game. It is always victorious when properly played.

It is the players who are at fault. The great trouble with all failures is that they were not started right. It was not drilled into the very texture of their being in youth that what they would get out of life must be created mentally first, and that inside the man, inside the woman, is where the great creative processes of life are carried on.

That which man does with his hands is secondary. It is what he does with his brain that counts. That is what starts things going. Some of us never learn how to create with our minds. We depend too much upon creating with our hands, or on other people to help us. We depend too much on the things outside of us when the mainspring of life, the power that moves the world of men and things, is inside of us.

There are times when we cannot see the way ahead, when we seem to be completely enveloped in the fogs of discouragement, disappointment and failure of our plans, but we can always do the thing that means salvation for us, that is persistently, determinedly, everlastingly to face towards our goal whether we can see it or not. This is our only chance of overcoming our difficulties. If we turn about face, turn our back on our goal, we are headed toward disaster.

No matter how many obstacles may block your path, or how dark the way, if you look up, think up, and struggle up, you can't help succeeding.

Whatever you do for a living, whatever fortune or misfortune may come to you, hold the victorious attitude and push ahead.

A captain might as well turn about his ship when he strikes a fog bank, because he cannot see the way ahead of him, and still expect to make his distant harbor, as for you to drop your victorious attitude and face the other way just because you have run into a fog bank of disappointment or failure. The only hope of the captain's reaching his destination is in being true to the compass that guides him in the fog and darkness as well as in the light. He may not see the way, but he can follow his compass. That we also can do by holding the victorious attitude towards life, the only attitude that can insure safety and bring us into port.

- Happiness is not a matter of intensity but of balance, order, rhythm and harmony.
- Believe with all your heart that you will do what you were made to do.
- Most obstacles melt away when we make up our minds to walk boldly through them.
- Money, influence, and position are nothing compared with brains, principles, energy and perseverance.
- Personal nobility is greater than any calling, or any reward that it can bring.

FOUR

How to Make Best Use of Your Money

Andrew Carnegie answers from *The Gospel of Wealth*

Scottish-born Andrew Carnegie (1835-1919) was an American industrialist who amassed a fortune in the steel industry, then became a major philanthropist. The 'Gospel of Wealth' was an article written by him in 1889 wherein he argued that very wealthy men like him had a responsibility to use their wealth for the greater good of society.

T he problem of our age is the proper administration of wealth, so that the ties of brotherhood may still bind together the rich and poor in harmonious relationship. The conditions of human life have not only been changed, but revolutionized, within the past few hundred years. In former days there was little difference between the dwelling, dress, food and environment of the chief and those of his retainers. The Indians are today where civilized <u>man</u> then was. When visiting the Sioux, I was led to the wigwam of the chief. It was just like the others in external appearance, and even within the difference was trifling between it and those of the poorest of his braves. The contrast between the palace of the millionaire and the cottage of the laborer with us to-day measures the change which has come with civilization.

This change, however, is not to be deplored, but welcomed as highly beneficial. It is well, nay, essential for the progress of the race, that the houses of some should be homes for all that is highest and best in literature and the arts, and for all the refinements of civilization, rather than that none should be so. Much better this great irregularity than universal squalor. Without wealth there can be no Mæcenas. The "good old times" were not good old times. Neither master nor servant was as well situated then as to-day. A relapse to old conditions would be disastrous to both—not the least so to him who serves—and would sweep away civilization with it. But, whether the change be for good or ill, it is upon us, beyond our power to alter, and therefore to be accepted and made the best of. It is a waste of time to criticize the inevitable.

It is easy to see how the change has come. One illustration will serve for almost every phase of the cause. In the manufacture of products we have the whole story. It applies to all combinations of human industry, as stimulated and enlarged by the inventions of this scientific age. Formerly articles were manufactured at the domestic hearth or in small shops which formed part of the household. The master and his apprentices worked side by side, the latter living with the master, and therefore subject to the same conditions. When these apprentices rose to be masters, there was little or no change in their <u>mode</u> of life, and they, in turn, educated in the same routine succeeding apprentices. There was, substantially social equality, and even political equality, for those engaged in industrial pursuits had then little or no political voice in the State.

But, the inevitable result of such a mode of manufacture was crude articles at high prices. Today the world obtains commodities of excellent quality at prices which even the generation preceding this would have deemed incredible. In the commercial world similar causes have produced similar results, and the race is benefited thereby. The poor enjoy what the rich could not before afford. What were the luxuries have become the necessaries of life. The laborer has now more comforts than the landlord had a few generations ago. The farmer has more luxuries than the landlord had, and is more richly clad and better housed. The landlord has books and pictures rarer, and appointments more artistic, than the King could then obtain.

The price we pay for this salutary change is, no doubt, great. We assemble thousands of operatives in the factory, in the mine and in the counting-house, of whom the employer can know little or nothing, and to whom the employer is little better than a myth. All intercourse between them is at an end. Rigid castes are formed, and, as usual, mutual ignorance breeds mutual distrust. Each caste is without sympathy for the other and ready to credit anything disparaging in regard to it. Under the law of competition, the employer of thousands is forced into the strictest economies, among which the rates paid to labor figure prominently, and often there is friction between the employer and the employed, between capital and labor, between rich and poor. Human society loses homogeneity.

The price which society pays for the law of competition, like the price it pays for cheap comforts and luxuries, is also great; but the advantage of this law are also greater still, for it is to this law that we owe our wonderful material development, which brings improved conditions in its train. But, whether the law be benign or not, we must say of it, as we say of the change in the conditions of men to which we have referred: It is here; we cannot evade it; no substitutes for it have been found; and while the law may be sometimes hard for the individual, it is best for the race, because it insures the survival of the fittest in every department. We accept and welcome therefore, as conditions to which we must accommodate ourselves, great inequality of environment, the concentration of business, industrial and commercial, in the hands of a few, and the law of competition between these, as being not only beneficial, but essential for the future progress of the race. Having accepted these, it follows that there must be great scope for the exercise of special ability in the merchant and in the manufacturer who has to conduct affairs upon a great scale. That this talent for organization and management is rare among men is proved by the fact that it invariably secures for its possessor enormous rewards, no matter where or under what laws or conditions. The experienced in affairs always rate the MAN whose services can be obtained as a partner as not only the first consideration, but such as to render the question of his capital scarcely worth considering, for such men soon create capital; while, without the special talent required, capital soon takes wings. Such men become interested in firms or corporations using millions; and estimating only simple interest to be made upon the capital invested, it is inevitable that their income must exceed their expenditures and that they must accumulate wealth. Nor is there any middle ground which such men can occupy, because the great manufacturing or commercial concern which does not earn at least interest upon its capital soon becomes bankrupt. It, must either go forward or fall behind: to stand still is impossible. It is a condition essential for its successful operation that it should be thus far profitable, and even that, in addition to interest on capital, it should make profit. It is a law, as certain as any of the others named, that men possessed of this peculiar talent for affair, under the free play of economic forces, must, of necessity, soon be in receipt of more revenue than can be judiciously expended upon themselves; and this law is as beneficial for the race as the others.

Objections to the foundations upon which society is based are not in order, because the condition of the race is better with these than it has been with any others which have been tried. Of the effect of any new substitutes proposed we cannot be sure. The Socialist or Anarchist who seeks to overturn present conditions is to be regarded as attacking the foundation upon which civilization itself rests, for civilization took its start from the day that the capable, industrious workman said to his incompetent and lazy fellow, "If thou dost net sow, thou shalt net reap," and thus ended primitive Communism by separating the drones from the bees. One who studies this subject will soon be brought face to face with the conclusion that upon the sacredness of property civilization itself depends—the right of the laborer to his hundred dollars in the savings bank, and equally the legal right of the millionaire to his millions. To these who propose to substitute Communism for this intense Individualism, the answer, therefore, is: The race has tried that. All progress from that barbarous day to the present time has resulted from its displacement. Not evil, but good, has come to the race from the accumulation of wealth by those who have the ability and energy that produce it. But, even if we admit for a moment that it might be better for the race to discard its present foundation, Individualism—that it is a nobler ideal that man should labor, not for himself alone, but in and for a brotherhood of his fellows, and share with them all in common, realizing Swedenborg's idea of Heaven, where, as he says, the angels derive their happiness, not from laboring for self, but for each other—even admit all this, and a sufficient answer is, "This is not evolution, but revolution." It necessitates the changing of human nature itself a work of oeons, even if it were good to change it, which we cannot know. It is not practicable in our day or in our age. Even if desirable theoretically, it belongs to another and long-succeeding sociological stratum. Our duty is with what is practicable now; with the next step possible in our day and generation. It is criminal to waste our energies in endeavoring to uproot, when all we can profitably or possibly accomplish is to bend the universal tree of humanity a little in the direction most favorable to the production of good fruit under existing circumstances. We might as well urge the destruction of the highest existing type of man because he failed to reach our ideal as favor the destruction of Individualism, Private Property, the Law of Accumulation of Wealth, and the Law of Competition; for these are the highest results of human experience, the soil in which society so far has produced the best fruit. Unequally or unjustly, perhaps, as these laws sometimes operate, and imperfect as they appear to the Idealist, they are, nevertheless, like the highest type of man, the best and most valuable of all that humanity has yet accomplished.

We start, then, with a condition of affairs under which the best interests of the race are promoted, but which inevitably gives wealth to the few. Thus far, accepting conditions as they exist, the situation can be surveyed and pronounced good. The question then arises—and, if the foregoing be correct, it is the only question with which we have to deal—What is the proper mode of administering wealth after the laws upon which civilization is founded have thrown it into the hands of the few? And it is of this great question that I believe I offer the true solution. It will be understood that *fortunes* are here spoken of, not moderate sums saved by many years of effort, the returns on which are required for the comfortable maintenance and education of families. This is not *wealth*, but only *competence* which it should be the aim of all to acquire.

There are but three modes in which surplus wealth

can be disposed of. It can be left to the families of the decedents; or it can be bequeathed for public purposes; or, finally, it can be administered during their lives by its possessors. Under the first and second modes most of the wealth of the world that has reached the few has hitherto been applied. Let us in turn consider each of these modes. The first is the most injudicious. In monarchical countries, the estates and the greatest portion of the wealth are left to the first son, that the vanity of the parent may be gratified by the thought that his name and title are to descend to succeeding generations unimpaired. The condition of this class in Europe today teaches the futility of such hopes or ambitions. The successors have become impoverished through their follies or from the fall in the value of land. Even in Great Britain the strict law of entail has been found inadequate to maintain the status of a hereditary class. Its soil is rapidly passing into the hands of the stranger. Under republican institutions the division of property among the children is much fairer, but the question that forces itself upon thoughtful men in all lands is: Why should men leave great fortunes to their children? If this is done from affection, is it not misguided affection? Observation teaches that, generally speaking, it is not well for the children that they should be so burdened. Neither is it well for the state. Beyond providing for the wife and daughters moderate sources of income, and very moderate allowances indeed, if any, for the sons, men may well hesitate, for it is no longer questionable that great suns bequeathed oftener work more for the injury than for the good of the recipients. Wise men will soon conclude that, for the best interests of the members of their families and of the state, such bequests are an improper use of their means.

It is not suggested that men who have failed to educate their sons to earn a livelihood shall cast them adrift in poverty. If any man has seen fit to rear his sons with a view to their living idle lives, or, what is highly commendable, has instilled in them the sentiment that they are in a position to labor for public ends without reference to pecuniary considerations, then, of course, the duty of the parent is to see that such are provided for in moderation. There are instances of millionaires' sons unspoiled by wealth, who, being rich, still perform great services in the community. Such are the very salt of the earth, as valuable as, unfortunately, they are rare; still it is not the exception, but the rule, that men must regard, and looking at the usual result of enormous sums conferred upon legatees, the thoughtful man must shortly say, "I would as soon leave to my son a curse as the almighty dollar," and admit to himself that it is not the welfare of the children, but family pride, which inspires these enormous legacies.

As to the second mode, that of leaving wealth at death for public uses, it may be said that this is only a means for the disposal of wealth, provided a man is content to wait until he is dead before it becomes of much good in the world. Knowledge of the results of legacies bequeathed is not calculated to inspire the brightest hopes of much posthumous good being accomplished. The cases are not few in which the real object sought by the testator is not attained, nor are they few in which his real wishes are thwarted. In many cases the bequests are so used as to become only monuments of his folly. It is well to remember that it requires the exercise of not less ability than that which acquired the wealth to use it so as to be really beneficial to the community. Besides this, it may fairly be said that no man is to be extolled for doing what he cannot help doing, nor is he to be thanked by the community to which he only leaves wealth at death. Men who leave vast sums in this way may fairly be thought men who would not have left it at all, had they been able to take it with them. The memories of such cannot be held in grateful remembrance, for there is no grace in their gifts. It is not to be wondered at that such bequests seem so generally to lack the blessing.

The growing disposition to tax more and more heavily large estates left at death is a cheering indication of the growth of a salutary change in public opinion. The State of Pennsylvania now takes—subject to some exceptions— one-tenth of the property left by its citizens. The budget presented in the British Parliament the other day proposes to increase the death-duties; and, most significant of all, the new tax is to be a graduated one. Of all forms of taxation, this seems the wisest. Men who continue hoarding great sums all their lives, the proper use of which for—public ends would work good to the community, should be made to feel that the community, in the form of the state, cannot thus be deprived of its proper share. By taxing estates heavily at death the state marks its condemnation of the selfish millionaire's unworthy life.

It is desirable;that nations should go much further in this direction. Indeed, it is difficult to set bounds to the share of a rich man's estate which should go at his death to the public through the agency of the state, and by all means such taxes should be graduated, beginning at nothing upon moderate sums to dependents, and increasing rapidly as the amounts swell, until of the millionaire's hoard, as of Shylock's, at least

"______ The other half
Comes to the privy coffer of the state."

This policy would work powerfully to induce the rich man to attend to the administration of wealth during his life, which is the end that society should always have in view, as being that by far most fruitful for the people. Nor need it be feared that this policy would sap the root of enterprise and render men less anxious to accumulate, for to the class whose ambition it is to leave great fortunes and be talked about after their death, it will attract even more attention, and, indeed, be a somewhat nobler ambition to have enormous sums paid over to the state from their fortunes.

There remains, then, only one mode of using great fortunes; but in this we have the true antidote for the temporary unequal distribution of wealth, the reconciliation of the rich and the poor—a reign of harmony—another ideal, differing, indeed, from that of the Communist in requiring only the further evolution of existing conditions, not the total overthrow of our civilization. It is founded upon the present most intense individualism, and the race is projected to put it in practice by degree whenever it pleases. Under its sway we shall have an ideal state, in which the surplus wealth of the few will become, in the best sense the property of the many, because administered for the common good, and this wealth, passing through the hands of the few, can be made a much more potent force for the elevation of our race than if it had been distributed in small sums to the people themselves. Even the poorest can be made to see this, and to agree that great sums gathered by some of their fellow-citizens and spent for public purposes, from which the masses reap the principal benefit, are more valuable to them than if scattered among them through the course of many years in trifling amounts.

If we consider what results flow from the Cooper Institute, for instance, to the best portion of the race in New York not possessed of means, and compare these with those which would have arisen for the good of the masses from an equal sum distributed by Mr. Cooper in his lifetime in the form of wages, which is the highest form of distribution, being for work done and not for charity, we can form some estimate of the possibilities for the improvement of the race which lie embedded in the present law of the accumulation of wealth. Much of this sum if distributed in small quantities among the people, would have been wasted in the indulgence of appetite, some of it in excess, and it may be doubted whether even the part put to the best use,that of adding to the comforts of the home, would have yielded results for the race, as a race, at all comparable to those which are flowing and are to flow from the Cooper Institute from generation to generation. Let the advocate of violent or radical change ponder well this thought.

We might even go so far as to take another instance, that of Mr. Tilden's bequest of 5 millions of dollars for a free library in the city of New York, but in referring to this one cannot help saying involuntarily, how much better if Mr. Tilden had devoted the last years of his own life to the proper administration of this immense sum; in which case neither legal contest nor any other cause of delay could have interfered with his aims. But, let us assume that Mr. Tilden's millions finally become the means of giving to this city a noble public library, where the treasures of the world contained in books will be open to all forever, without money and without price. Considering the good of that part of the race which congregates in and around Manhattan Island, would its permanent benefit have been better promoted had these millions been allowed to circulate in small sums through the hands of the masses? Even the most strenuous advocate of Communism must entertain a doubt upon this subject. Most of those who think will probably entertain no doubt whatever.

Poor and restricted are our opportunities in this life; narrow our horizon; our best work most imperfect; but rich men should be thankful for one inestimable boon. They have it in their power during their lives to busy themselves in organizing benefactions from which the masses of their fellows will derive lasting advantage, and thus dignify their own lives. The highest life is probably to be reached, not by such imitation of the life of Christ as Count Tolstoi gives us, but, while animated by Christ's spirit, by recognizing the changed conditions of this age, and adopting modes of expressing this spirit suitable to the changed conditions under which we live; still laboring for the good of our fellows, which was the essence of his life and teaching, but laboring in a different manner.

This, then, is held to be the duty of the man of Wealth: First, to set an example of modest, unostentatious living, shunning display or extravagance; to provide moderately for the legitimate wants of those dependent upon him; and after doing so to consider all surplus revenues which come to him simply as trust funds, which he is called upon to administer, and strictly bound as a matter of duty to administer in the manner which, in his judgment, is best calculated to produce the most beneficial results for the community—the man of wealth thus becoming the mere agent and trustee for his poorer brethren, bringing to their service his superior wisdom, experience and ability to administer, doing for them better than they would or could do for themselves.

We are met here with the difficulty of determining what are moderate sums to leave to members of the family; what is modest, unostentatious living; what is the test of extravagance. There must be different standards for different conditions. The answer is that it is as impossible to name exact amounts or actions as it is to define good manners, good taste or the rules of propriety; but, nevertheless, these are verities, well-known although undefinable. Public sentiment is quick to know and to feel what offends these. So in the case of wealth. The rule in regard to good taste in the dress of men or women applies here. Whatever makes one conspicuous offends the canon. If any family be chiefly known for display, for extravagance in home, table, equipage, for enormous sums ostentatiously spent in any form upon itself, if these be its chief distinctions, we have no difficulty in estimating its nature or culture. So likewise in regard to the use or abuse of its surplus wealth, or to generous, free-handed cooperation in good public uses, or to unabated efforts to accumulate and hoard to the last, whether they administer or bequeath. The verdict rests with the best and most enlightened public sentiment. The community will surely judge and its judgments will not often be wrong.

The best uses to which surplus wealth can be put have already been indicated. These who would administer wisely must, indeed, be wise, for one of the serious obstacles to the improvement of our race is indiscriminate charity. It were better for mankind that the millions of the rich were thrown in to the sea than so spent as to encourage the slothful, the drunken, the unworthy. Of every thousand dollars spent in so called charity to-day, it is probable that $950 is unwisely spent; so spent, indeed as to produce the very evils which it proposes to mitigate or cure. A well-known writer of philosophic books admitted the other day that he had given a quarter of a dollar to a man who approached him as he was coming to visit the house of his friend. He knew nothing of the habits of this beggar;

knew not the use that would be made of this money, although he had every reason to suspect that it would be spent improperly. This man professed to be a disciple of Herbert Spencer; yet the quarter-dollar given that night will probably work more injury than all the money which its thoughtless donor will ever be able to give in true charity will do good.

He only gratified his own feelings, saved him- self from annoyance—and this was probably one of the most selfish and very worst actions of his life, for in all respects he is most worthy.

In bestowing charity, the main consideration should be to help those who will help themselves; to provide part of the means by which those who desire to improve may do so; to give those who desire to use the aids by which they may rise; to assist, but rarely or never to do all. Neither the individual nor the race is improved by alms-giving.

Those worthy of assistance, except in rare cases, seldom require assistance. The really valuable men of the race never do, except in cases of accident or sudden change. Every one has, of course, cases of individuals brought to his own knowledge where temporary assistance can do genuine good, and these he will not overlook. But, the amount which can be wisely given by the individual for individuals is necessarily limited by his lack of knowledge of the circumstances connected with each. He is the only true reformer who is as careful and as anxious not to aid the unworthy as he is to aid the worthy, and, perhaps, even more so, for in alms-giving more injury is probably done by rewarding vice than by relieving virtue.

The rich man is thus almost restricted to following the examples of Peter Cooper, Enoch Pratt of Baltimore, Mr. Pratt of Brooklyn, Senator Stanford and others, who know that the best means of benefiting the community is to place within its reach the ladders upon which the aspiring can rise—parks, and means of recreation, by which men are helped in body and mind; works of art, certain to give pleasure and improve the public taste, and public institutions of various kinds, which will improve the general condition of the people—in this manner returning their surplus wealth to the mass of their fellows in the forms best calculated to do them lasting good.

Thus is the problem of Rich and Poor to be solved. The laws of accumulation will be left free; the laws of distribution free. Individualism will continue, but the millionaire will be but a trustee for the poor; intrusted for a season with a great part of the increased wealth of the community, but administering it for the community far better than it could or would have done for itself. The best minds will thus have reached a stage in the development of the race in which it is clearly seen that there is no mode of disposing of surplus wealth creditable to thoughtful and earnest men into whose hands it flows save by using it year by year for the general good. This day already dawns. But, a little while, and although, without incurring the pity of their fellows, men may die sharers in great business enterprises from which their capital cannot be or has not been withdrawn, and is left chiefly at death for public uses, yet the man who dies leaving behind many millions of available wealth, which was his to administer during life, will pass away "unwept, unhonored, and unsung," no matter to what uses he leaves the dross which he cannot take with him. Of such as these the public verdict will then be: "The man who dies thus rich dies disgraced."

Such, in my opinion, is the true Gospel concerning Wealth, obedience to which is destined someday to solve the problem of the Rich and the Poor, and to bring "Peace on earth, among men Good-Will."

- "It is a waste of time to criticize the inevitable."
- The real value of money relies on its proper distribution.
- The rich must follow a humble lifestyle and have a positive social image.
- Proper oversight is needed; else recipients will mishandle charity.
- Random acts of donation are often ineffective. They don't benefit the full society.

FIVE

How to Make Sense of the Daily Chaos of Life

Marcus Aurelius answers from *Meditations*

Meditations is a collection of personal notes written by the author, Marcus Aurelius (121 A.D.—180 A.D.), to himself. These notes were never intended for publication and had two purposes: To define for himself a life philosophy and an ideal character worthy of aspiring to.

∿

A man must not only consider how daily his life wasteth and decreaseth, but this also, that if he live long, he cannot be certain, whether his understanding shall continue so able and sufficient, for either discreet consideration, in matter of businesses; or for contemplation: it being the thing, whereon true knowledge of things both divine and human, doth depend. For if once he shall begin to dote, his respiration, nutrition, his imaginative, and appetitive, and other natural faculties, may still continue the same: he shall find no want of them. But how to make that right use of himself that he should, how to observe exactly in all things that which is right and just, how to redress and rectify all wrong, or sudden apprehensions and imaginations, and even of this particular, whether he should live any longer or no, to consider duly; for all such things, wherein the best strength and vigour of the mind is most requisite; his power and ability will be past and gone. Thou must hasten therefore; not only because thou art every day nearer unto death than other, but also because that intellective faculty in thee, whereby thou art enabled to know the true nature of things, and to order all thy actions by that knowledge, doth daily waste and decay: or, may fail thee before thou die.

This also thou must observe, that whatsoever it is that naturally doth happen to things natural, hath somewhat in itself that is pleasing and delightful: as a great loaf when it is baked, some parts of it cleave as it were, and part asunder, and make the crust of it rugged and unequal, and yet those parts of it, though in some sort it be against the art and intention of baking itself, that they are thus cleft and parted, which should have been and were first made all even and uniform, they become it well nevertheless, and have a certain peculiar property, to stir the appetite. So figs are accounted fairest and ripest then, when they begin to shrink, and wither as it were. So ripe olives, when they are next to putrefaction, then are they in their proper beauty. The hanging down of grapes—the brow of a lion, the froth of a foaming wild boar, and many other like things, though by themselves considered, they are far from any beauty, yet because they happen naturally, they both are comely, and delightful; so that if a man shall with a profound mind and apprehension, consider all things in the world, even among all those things which are but mere accessories and natural appendices as it were, there will scarce appear anything unto him, wherein he will not find matter of pleasure and delight. So will he behold with as much pleasure the true rictus of wild beasts, as those which by skilful painters and other artificers are imitated. So will he be able to perceive the proper ripeness and beauty of old age, whether in man or woman: and whatsoever else it is that is beautiful and alluring in whatsoever is, with chaste and continent eyes he will soon find out and discern. Those and many other things will he discern, not credible unto every one, but unto them only who are truly and familiarly acquainted, both with nature itself, and all natural things.

Hippocrates having cured many sicknesses, fell sick himself and died. The Chaldeans and Astrologians having foretold the deaths of divers, were afterwards themselves surprised by the fates. Alexander and Pompeius, and Caius Caesar, having destroyed so many towns, and cut off in the field so many thousands both of horse and foot, yet they themselves at last were fain to part with their own lives. Heraclitus having written so many natural tracts concerning the last and general conflagration of the world, died afterwards all filled with water within, and all bedaubed with dirt and dung without. Lice killed Democritus; and Socrates, another sort of vermin, wicked ungodly men. How then stands the case? Thou hast taken ship, thou hast sailed, thou art come to land, go out, if to another life, there also shalt thou find gods, who are everywhere. If all life and sense shall cease, then shalt thou cease also to be subject to either pains or pleasures; and to serve and tend this vile cottage; so much the viler, by how much that which ministers unto it doth excel; the one being a rational substance, and a spirit, the other nothing but earth and blood.

Spend not the remnant of thy days in thoughts and fancies concerning other men, when it is not in relation to some common good, when by it thou art hindered from some other better work. That is, spend not thy time in thinking, what such a man doth, and to what end: what he saith, and what he thinks, and what he is about, and such other things or curiosities, which make a man to rove and wander from the care and observation of that part of himself, which is rational, and overruling. See therefore in the whole series and connection of thy thoughts, that thou be careful to prevent whatsoever is idle and impertinent: but especially, whatsoever is curious and malicious: and thou must use thyself to think only of such things, of which if a man upon a sudden should ask thee, what it is that thou art now thinking, thou mayest answer This, and That, freely and boldly, that so by thy thoughts it may presently appear that in all thee is sincere, and peaceable; as becometh one that is made for society, and regards not pleasures, nor gives way to any voluptuous imaginations at all: free from all contentiousness, envy, and suspicion, and from whatsoever else thou wouldest blush to confess thy thoughts were set upon. He that is such, is he surely that doth not put off to lay hold on that which is best indeed, a very priest and minister of the gods, well acquainted and in good correspondence with him especially that is seated and placed within himself, as in a temple and sacrary: to whom also he keeps and preserves himself unspotted by pleasure, undaunted by pain; free from any manner of wrong, or contumely, by himself offered unto himself: not capable of any evil from others: a wrestler of the best sort, and for the highest prize, that he may not be cast down by any passion or affection of his own; deeply dyed and drenched in righteousness, embracing and accepting with his whole heart whatsoever either happeneth or is allotted unto him. One who not often, nor without some great necessity tending to some public good, mindeth what any other, either speaks, or doth, or purposeth: for those things only that are in his own power, or that are truly his own, are the objects of his employments, and his thoughts are ever taken up with those things, which of the whole universe are by the fates or Providence destinated and appropriated unto himself. Those things that are his own, and in his own power, he himself takes order, for that they be good: and as for those that happen unto him, he believes them to be so. For that lot and portion which is assigned to every one, as it is unavoidable and necessary, so is it always profitable. He remembers besides that whatsoever partakes of reason, is akin unto him, and that to care for all men generally, is agreeing to the nature of a man: but as for honour and praise, that they ought not generally to be admitted and accepted of from all, but from such only, who live according to nature. As for them that do not, what manner of men they be at home, or abroad; day or night, how conditioned themselves with what manner of conditions, or with men of what conditions they moil and pass away the time together, he knoweth, and remembers right well, he therefore regards not such praise and approbation, as proceeding from them, who cannot like and approve themselves.

Do nothing against thy will, nor contrary to the

community, nor without due examination, nor with reluctancy. Affect not to set out thy thoughts with curious neat language. Be neither a great talker, nor a great undertaker. Moreover, let thy God that is in thee to rule over thee, find by thee, that he hath to do with a man; an aged man; a sociable man; a Roman; a prince; one that hath ordered his life, as one that expecteth, as it were, nothing but the sound of the trumpet, sounding a retreat to depart out of this life with all expedition. One who for his word or actions neither needs an oath, nor any man to be a witness.

To be cheerful, and to stand in no need, either of other men's help or attendance, or of that rest and tranquillity, which thou must be beholding to others for. Rather like one that is straight of himself, or hath ever been straight, than one that hath been rectified.

If thou shalt find anything in this mortal life better than righteousness, than truth, temperance, fortitude, and in general better than a mind contented both with those things which according to right and reason she doth, and in those, which without her will and knowledge happen unto thee by the providence; if I say, thou canst find out anything better than this, apply thyself unto it with thy whole heart, and that which is best wheresoever thou dost find it, enjoy freely. But if nothing thou shalt find worthy to be preferred to that spirit which is within thee; if nothing better than to subject unto thee thine own lusts and desires, and not to give way to any fancies or imaginations before thou hast duly considered of them, nothing better than to withdraw thyself (to use Socrates his words) from all sensuality, and submit thyself unto the gods, and to have care of all men in general: if thou shalt find that all other things in comparison of this, are but vile, and of little moment; then give not way to any other thing, which being once though but affected and inclined unto, it will no more be in thy power without all distraction as thou oughtest to prefer and to pursue after that good, which is thine own and thy proper good. For it is not lawful, that anything that is of another and inferior kind and nature, be it what it will, as either popular applause, or honour, or riches, or pleasures; should be suffered to confront and contest as it were, with that which is rational, and operatively good. For all these things, if once though but for a while, they begin to please, they presently prevail, and pervert a man's mind, or turn a man from the right way. Do thou therefore I say absolutely and freely make choice of that which is best, and stick unto it. Now, that they say is best, which is most profitable. If they mean profitable to man as he is a rational man, stand thou to it, and maintain it; but if they mean profitable, as he is a creature, only reject it; and from this thy tenet and conclusion keep off carefully all plausible shows and colours of external appearance, that thou mayest be able to discern things rightly.

Never esteem of anything as profitable, which shall ever constrain thee either to break thy faith, or to lose thy modesty; to hate any man, to suspect, to curse, to dissemble, to lust after anything, that requireth the secret of walls or veils. But he that preferreth before all things his rational part and spirit, and the sacred mysteries of virtue which issueth from it, he shall never lament and exclaim, never sigh; he shall never want either solitude or company: and which is chiefest of all, he shall live without either desire or fear. And as for life, whether for a long or short time he shall enjoy his soul thus compassed about with a body, he is altogether indifferent. For if even now he were to depart, he is as ready for it, as for any other action, which may be performed with modesty and decency. For all his life long, this is his only care, that his mind may always be occupied in such intentions and objects, as are proper to a rational sociable creature.

In the mind that is once truly disciplined and purged, thou canst not find anything, either foul or impure, or as it were festered: nothing that is either servile, or affected: no partial tie; no malicious averseness; nothing obnoxious; nothing concealed. The life of such an one, death can never surprise as imperfect; as of an actor, that should die before he had ended, or the play itself were at an end, a man might speak.

Use thine opinative faculty with all honour and respect,

for in her indeed is all: that thy opinion do not beget in thy understanding anything contrary to either nature, or the proper constitution of a rational creature. The end and object of a rational constitution is, to do nothing rashly, to be kindly affected towards men, and in all things willingly to submit unto the gods. Casting therefore all other things aside, keep thyself to these few, and remember withal that no man properly can be said to live more than that which is now present, which is but a moment of time. Whatsoever is besides either is already past, or uncertain. The time therefore that any man doth live, is but a little, and the place where he liveth, is but a very little corner of the earth, and the greatest fame that can remain of a man after his death, even that is but little, and that too, such as it is whilst it is, is by the succession of silly mortal men preserved, who likewise shall shortly die, and even whiles they live know not what in very deed they themselves are: and much less can know one, who long before is dead and gone.

To these ever-present helps and mementoes, let one more be added, ever to make a particular description and delineation as it were of every object that presents itself to thy mind, that thou mayest wholly and throughly contemplate it, in its own proper nature, bare and naked; wholly, and severally; divided into its several parts and quarters: and then by thyself in thy mind, to call both it, and those things of which it doth consist, and in which it shall be resolved, by their own proper true names, and appellations. For there is nothing so effectual to beget true magnanimity, as to be able truly and methodically to examine and consider all things that happen in this life, and so to penetrate into their natures, that at the same time, this also may concur in our apprehensions: what is the true use of it? and what is the true nature of this universe, to which it is useful? how much in regard of the universe may it be esteemed? how much in regard of man, a citizen of the supreme city, of which all other cities in the world are as it were but houses and families?

- The evil that men do harms you only if you do evil in response.
- Do not try to escape other people's faults. They are inescapable. Try to escape your own.
- Fame and desires are not worth pursuing.
- Death will always overshadow you. So don't live as if you have endless years. While you're alive and able—be good.
- The future things will come to you if necessary. It is pointless to think and fret about "what's in store for us".

SIX

How to Draw Inspiration from Failures

Boethius answers from *The Consolation of philosophy*

For some 400 years across the European Middle Ages, one philosophy book was prized above any other. Present in every educated person's library, it was titled in Latin *De Consolatione Philosophiae* or, as we know it in English today, The Consolation of Philosophy.

The influence of each area of Boethius's philosophical writing was vast in the Middle Ages. Along with Augustine and Aristotle, he is the fundamental philosophical and theological author in the Latin tradition.

Boethius (477–524 A.D.) may have written his book, The Consolation of Philosophy, *from prison in the year 524 AD, but the issues he addresses are every bit as relevant to modern life as they were to life in the 6th century. A philosopher, statesman, and theologian, Boethius was imprisoned by Germanic King Theoderick on trumped up charges. Consolation is written in an elaborate literary form: it consists of a dialogue between Boethius, sitting in his prison-cell awaiting execution, and a lady who personifies philosophy, and its often highly rhetorical prose is interspersed with verse passages.*

What is it, then, poor mortal, that hath cast thee into lamentation and mourning? Some strange, unwonted sight, methinks, have thine eyes seen. Thou deemest Fortune to have changed towards thee; thou mistakest. Such ever were her ways, ever such her nature. Rather in her very mutability hath she preserved towards thee her true constancy. Such was she when she loaded thee with caresses, when she deluded thee with the allurements of a false happiness. Thou hast found out how changeful is the face of the blind goddess. She who still veils herself from others hath fully discovered to thee her whole character. If thou likest her, take her as she is, and do not complain. If thou abhorrest her perfidy, turn from her in disdain, renounce her, for baneful are her delusions. The very thing which is now the cause of thy great grief ought to have brought thee tranquillity. Thou hast been forsaken by one of whom no one can be sure that she will not forsake him. Or dost thou indeed set value on a happiness that is certain to depart? Again I ask, Is Fortune's presence dear to thee if she cannot be trusted to stay, and though she will bring sorrow when she is gone? Why, if she cannot be kept at pleasure, and if her flight overwhelms with calamity, what is this fleeting visitant but a token of coming trouble? Truly it is not enough to look only at what lies before the eyes; wisdom gauges the issues of things, and this same mutability, with its two aspects, makes the threats of Fortune void of terror, and her caresses little to be desired. Finally, thou oughtest to bear with whatever takes place within the boundaries of Fortune's demesne, when thou hast placed thy head beneath her yoke. But if thou wishest to impose a law of staying and departing on her whom thou hast of thine own accord chosen for thy mistress, art thou not acting wrongfully, art thou not embittering by impatience a lot which thou canst not alter? Didst thou commit thy sails to the winds, thou wouldst voyage not whither thy intention was to go, but whither the winds drave thee; didst thou entrust thy seed to the fields, thou wouldst set off the fruitful years against the barren. Thou hast resigned thyself to the sway of Fortune; thou must submit to thy mistress's caprices. What! art thou verily striving to stay the swing of the revolving wheel? Oh, stupidest of mortals, if it takes to standing still, it ceases to be the wheel of Fortune.'

'All mortal creatures in those anxious aims which find employment in so many varied pursuits, though they take many paths, yet strive to reach one goal—the goal of happiness. Now, *the good* is that which, when a man hath got, he can lack nothing further. This it is which is the supreme good of all, containing within itself all particular good; so that if anything is still wanting thereto, this cannot be the supreme good, since something would be left outside which might be desired. 'Tis clear, then, that happiness is a state perfected by the assembling together of all good things. To this state, as we have said, all men try to attain, but by different paths. For the desire of the true good is naturally implanted in the minds of men; only error leads them aside out of the way in pursuit of the false. Some, deeming it the highest good to want for nothing, spare no pains to attain affluence; others, judging the good to be that to which respect is most worthily paid, strive to win the reverence of their fellow-citizens by the attainment of official dignity. Some there are who fix the chief good in supreme power; these either wish themselves to enjoy sovereignty, or try to attach themselves to those who have it. Those, again, who think renown to be something of supreme excellence are in haste to spread abroad the glory of their name either through the arts of war or of peace. A great many measure the attainment of good by joy and gladness of heart; these think it the height of happiness to give themselves over to pleasure. Others there are, again, who interchange the ends and means one with the other in their aims; for instance, some want riches for the sake of pleasure and power, some covet power either for the sake of money or in order to bring renown to their name. So it is on these ends, then, that the aim of human acts and wishes is centred, and on others like to these—for instance, noble birth and popularity, which seem to compass a certain renown; wife and children, which are sought for the sweetness of their possession; while as for friendship, the most sacred kind indeed is counted in the category of virtue, not of fortune; but other kinds are entered upon for the sake of power or of enjoyment. And as for bodily excellences, it is obvious that they are to be ranged with the above. For strength and stature surely manifest power; beauty and fleetness of foot bring celebrity; health brings pleasure. It is plain, then, that the only object sought for in all these ways is *happiness*. For that which each seeks in preference to all else, that is in his judgment the supreme good. And we have defined the supreme good to be happiness. Therefore, that state which each wishes in preference to all others is in his judgment happy.

Thou seest, then, in what foulness unrighteous deeds are

sunk, with what splendour righteousness shines. Whereby it is manifest that goodness never lacks its reward, nor crime its punishment. For, verily, in all manner of transactions that for the sake of which the particular action is done may justly be accounted the reward of that action, even as the wreath for the sake of which the race is run is the reward offered for running. Now, we have shown happiness to be that very good for the sake of which all human actions. But, truly, this is a reward from which it is impossible to separate things are done. Absolute good, then, is offered as the common prize, as it were, of all the good man, for one who is without good cannot properly be called good at all; wherefore righteous dealing never misses its reward. Rage the wicked, then, never so violently, the crown shall not fall from the head of the wise, nor wither. Verily, other men's unrighteousness cannot pluck from righteous souls their proper glory. Were the reward in which the soul of the righteous delighteth received from without, then might it be taken away by him who gave it, or some other; but since it is conferred by his own righteousness, then only will he lose his prize when he has ceased to be righteous. Lastly, since every prize is desired because it is believed to be good, who can account him who possesses good to be without reward? And what a prize, the fairest and grandest of all! For remember the corollary which I chiefly insisted on a little while back, and reason thus: Since absolute good is happiness, 'tis clear that all the good must be happy for the very reason that they are good. But it was agreed that those who are happy are gods. So, then, the prize of the good is one which no time may impair, no man's power lessen, no man's unrighteousness tarnish; 'tis very Godship. And this being so, the wise man cannot doubt that punishment is inseparable from the bad. For since good and bad, and likewise reward and punishment, are contraries, it necessarily follows that, corresponding to all that we see accrue as reward of the good, there is some penalty attached as punishment of evil. As, then, righteousness itself is the reward of the righteous, so wickedness itself is the punishment of the unrighteous. Now, no one who is visited with punishment doubts that he is visited with evil. Accordingly, if they were but willing to weigh their own case, could they think themselves free from punishment whom wickedness, worst of all evils, has not only touched, but deeply tainted?

See, also, from the opposite standpoint—the standpoint of the good—what a penalty attends upon the wicked. Thou didst learn a little since that whatever is is one, and that unity itself is good. Accordingly, by this way of reckoning, whatever falls away from goodness ceases to be; whence it comes to pass that the bad cease to be what they were, while only the outward aspect is still left to show they have been men. Wherefore, by their perversion to badness, they have lost their true human nature. Further, since righteousness alone can raise men above the level of humanity, it must needs be that unrighteousness degrades below man's level those whom it has cast out of man's estate. It results, then, that thou canst not consider him human whom thou seest transformed by vice. The violent despoiler of other men's goods, enflamed with covetousness, surely resembles a wolf. A bold and restless spirit, ever wrangling in law-courts, is like some yelping cur. The secret schemer, taking pleasure in fraud and stealth, is own brother to the fox. The passionate man, phrenzied with rage, we might believe to be animated with the soul of a lion. The coward and runaway, afraid where no fear is, may be likened to the timid deer. He who is sunk in ignorance and stupidity lives like a dull ass. He who is light and inconstant, never holding long to one thing, is for all the world like a bird. He who wallows in foul and unclean lusts is sunk in the pleasures of a filthy hog. So it comes to pass that he who by forsaking righteousness ceases to be a man cannot pass into a Godlike condition, but actually turns into a brute beast.'

- ◆ "The reckless forces of folly" will never triumph in the end.
- ◆ One needs to find a truth more durable than any passing mood to sustain through life's up's and downs.
- ◆ You are wrong if you think Fortune has changed toward you. Change is Fortunes normal behavior, her true nature.
- ◆ Good fortune deceives, but bad fortune enlightens.
- ◆ Mortal men travel by different paths, though all are striving to reach one and the same goal, namely, happiness.

SEVEN

How to Be Yourself in a World that Is Trying to Change You

Ralph Waldo Emerson answers from *Self-Reliance*

Published first in 1841 in Essays *and then in the 1847 revised edition of* Essays, *"Self-Reliance" took shape over a long period of time. Throughout his life, Emerson kept detailed journals of his thoughts and actions, and he returned to them as a source for many of his essays. Such is the case with "Self-Reliance," which includes materials from journal entries dating as far back as 1832. In addition to his journals, Emerson drew on various lectures he delivered between 1836 and 1839.*

"Man is his own star; and the soul that can Render an honest and a perfect man, Commands all light, all influence, all fate; Nothing to him falls early or too late. Our acts our

angels are, or good or ill, Our fatal shadows that walk by us still."

I read the other day some verses written by an eminent painter which were original and not conventional. The soul always hears an admonition in such lines, let the subject be what it may. The sentiment they instill is of more value than any thought they may contain. To believe your own thought, to believe that what is true for you in your private heart is true for all men,—that is genius. Speak your latent conviction, and it shall be the universal sense; for the inmost in due time becomes the outmost,—and our first thought is rendered back to us by the trumpets of the Last Judgment. Familiar as the voice of the mind is to each, the highest merit we ascribe to Moses, Plato, and Milton is, that they set at naught books and traditions, and spoke not what men, but what they thought. A man should learn to detect and watch that gleam of light which flashes across his mind from within, more than the luster of the firmament of bards and sages. Yet he dismisses without notice his thought, because it is his. In every work of genius we recognize our own rejected thoughts: they come back to us with a certain alienated majesty. Great works of art have no more affecting lesson for us than this. They teach us to abide by our spontaneous impression with good-humored inflexibility then most when the whole cry of voices is on the other side. Else, tomorrow a stranger will say with masterly good sense precisely what we have thought and felt all the time, and we shall be forced to take with shame our own opinion from another.

There is a time in every man's education when he arrives at the conviction that envy is ignorance; that imitation is suicide; that he must take himself for better, for worse, as his portion; that though the wide universe is full of good, no kernel of nourishing corn can come to him but through his toil bestowed on that plot of ground which is given to him to till. The power which resides in him is new in nature, and none but he knows what that is which he can do, nor does he know until he has tried. Not for nothing one face, one character, one fact, makes much impression on him, and another none. This sculpture in the memory is not without preëstablished harmony. The eye was placed where one ray should fall, that it might testify of that particular ray. We but half express ourselves, and are ashamed of that divine idea which each of us represents. It may be safely trusted as proportionate and of good issues, so it be faithfully imparted, but God will not have his work made manifest by cowards. A man is relieved and gay when he has put his heart into his work and done his best; but what he has said or done otherwise shall give him no peace. It is a deliverance which does not deliver. In the attempt his genius deserts him; no muse befriends; no invention, no hope.

Trust thyself: every heart vibrates to that iron string. Accept the place the divine providence has found for you, the society of your contemporaries, the connection of events. Great men have always done so, and confided themselves childlike to the genius of their age, betraying their perception that the absolutely trustworthy was seated at their heart, working through their hands, predominating in all their being. And we are now men, and must accept in the highest mind the same transcendent destiny; and not minors and invalids in a protected corner, not cowards fleeing before a revolution, but guides, redeemers, and benefactors, obeying the Almighty effort, and advancing on Chaos and the Dark.

What pretty oracles nature yields us on this text, in the face and behavior of children, babes, and even brutes! That divided and rebel mind, that distrust of a sentiment because our arithmetic has computed the strength and means opposed to our purpose, these have not. Their mind being whole, their eye is as yet unconquered, and when we look in their faces we are disconcerted. Infancy conforms to nobody: all conform to it, so that one babe commonly makes four or five out of the adults who prattle and play to it. So God has armed youth and puberty and manhood no less with its own piquancy and charm, and made it enviable and gracious and its claims not to be put by, if it will stand by itself. Do not think the youth has no force, because he cannot speak to you and me. Hark! in the next room his voice is sufficiently clear and emphatic. It seems he knows how to speak to his contemporaries. Bashful or bold, then, he will know how to make us seniors very unnecessary.

The nonchalance of boys who are sure of a dinner, and would disdain as much as a lord to do or say aught to conciliate one, is the healthy attitude of human nature. A boy is in the parlor what the pit is in the playhouse; independent, irresponsible, looking out from his corner on such people and facts as pass by, he tries and sentences them on their merits, in the swift, summary way of boys, as good, bad, interesting, silly, eloquent, troublesome. He cumbers himself never about consequences about interests; he gives an independent, genuine verdict. You must court him: he does not court you. But the man is, as it were, clapped into jail by his consciousness. As soon as he has once acted or spoken with éclat he is a committed person, watched by the sympathy or the hatred of hundreds, whose affections must now enter into his account. There is no Lethe for this. Ah, that he could pass again into his neutrality! Who can thus avoid all pledges, and having observed, observe again from the same unaffected, unbiased, unbribable, unaffrighted innocence, must always be formidable. He would utter opinions on all passing affairs, which being seen to be not private, but necessary, would sink like darts into the ear of men, and put them in fear.

These are the voices which we hear in solitude, but they grow faint and inaudible as we enter into the world. Society everywhere is in conspiracy against the manhood of every one of its members. Society is a joint-stock company, in which the members agree, for the better securing of his bread to each shareholder, to surrender the liberty and culture of the eater. The virtue in most request is conformity. Self-reliance is its aversion. It loves not realities and creators, but names and customs.

Whoso would be a man must be a nonconformist. He who would gather immortal palms must not be hindered by the name of goodness, but must explore if it be goodness. Nothing is at last sacred but the integrity of your own mind. Absolve you to yourself, and you shall have the suffrage of the world. I remember an answer which when quite young I was prompted to make to a valued adviser, who was wont to importune me with the dear old doctrines of the is what is after my constitution, the only wrong what is against it. A man is to carry himself in the presence of all opposition, as if everything were titular and ephemeral but he. I am ashamed to think how easily we capitulate to badges and names, to large church. On my saying, What have I to do with the sacredness of traditions, if I live wholly from within? my friend suggested: "But these impulses may be from below, not from above." I replied: "They do not seem to me to be such; but if I am the Devil's child, I will live then from the Devil." No law can be sacred to me but that of my nature. Good and bad are but names very readily transferable to that or this; the only right societies and dead institutions. Every decent and well-spoken individual affects and sways me more than is right. I ought to go upright and vital, and speak the rude truth in all ways. If malice and vanity wear the coat of philanthropy, shall that pass? If an angry bigot assumes this bountiful cause of Abolition, and comes to me with his last news from Barbadoes, why should I not say to him: "Go love thy infant; love thy wood-chopper: be good-natured and modest: have that grace; and never varnish your hard, uncharitable ambition with this incredible tenderness for black folk a thousand miles off. Thy love afar is spite at home." Rough and graceless would be such greeting, but truth is handsomer than the affectation of love. Your goodness must have some edge to it,—else it is none. The doctrine of hatred must be preached as the counteraction of the doctrine of love when that pules and whines. I shun father and mother and wife and brother, when my genius calls me. I would write on the lintels of the door-post, Whim. I hope it is somewhat better than whim at last, but we cannot spend the day in explanation. Expect me not to show cause why I seek or why I exclude company. Then, again, do not tell me, as a good man did to-day, of my obligation to put all poor men in good situations. Are they my poor? I tell thee, thou foolish philanthropist, that I grudge the dollar, the dime, the cent, I give to such men as do not belong to me and to whom I do not belong. There is a class of persons to whom by all spiritual affinity I am bought and sold; for them I will go to prison, if need be; but your miscellaneous popular charities; the education at college of fools; the building of meeting-houses to the vain end to which many now stand; alms to sots; and the thousand-fold Relief Societies;—though I confess with shame I sometimes succumb and give the dollar, it is a wicked dollar which by and by I shall have the manhood to withhold.

Virtues are, in the popular estimate, rather the exception than the rule. There is the man and his virtues. Men do what is called a good action, as some piece of courage or charity, much as they would pay a fine in expiation of daily non-appearance on parade. Their works are done as an apology or extenuation of their living in the world,—as invalids and the insane pay a high board. Their virtues are penances. I do not wish to expiate, but to live. My life is for itself and not for a spectacle. I much prefer that it should be of a lower strain, so it be genuine and equal, than that it should be glittering and unsteady. I wish it to be sound and sweet, and not to need diet and bleeding. I ask primary evidence that you are a man, and refuse this appeal from the man to his actions. I know that for myself it makes no difference whether I do or forbear those actions which are reckoned excellent. I cannot consent to pay for a privilege where I have intrinsic right. Few and mean as my gifts may be, I actually am, and do not need for my own assurance or the assurance of my fellows any secondary testimony.

What I must do is all that concerns me, not what the people think. This rule, equally arduous in actual and in intellectual life, may serve for the whole distinction between greatness and meanness. It is the harder, because you will always find those who think they know what your duty is better than you know it. It is easy in the world to live after the world's opinion; it is easy in solitude to live after our own; but the great man is he who in the midst of the crowd keeps with perfect sweetness the independence of solitude.

The objection to conforming to usages that have become dead to you is, that it scatters your force. It loses your time and blurs the impression of your character. If you maintain a dead church, contribute to a dead Bible-society, vote with a great party either for the government or against it, spread your table like base housekeepers,—under all these screens I have difficulty to detect the precise man you are. And, of course, so much force is withdrawn from your proper life. But do your work, and I shall know you. Do your work, and you shall reinforce yourself. A man must consider what a blindman's-buff is this game of conformity. If I know your sect, I anticipate your argument. I hear a preacher announce for his text and topic the expediency of one of the institutions of his church. Do I not know beforehand that not possibly can he say a new and spontaneous word? Do I not know that, with all this ostentation of examining the grounds of the institution, he will do no such thing? Do I not know that he is pledged to himself not to look but at one side—the permitted side, not as a man, but as a parish minister? He is a retained attorney, and these airs of the bench are the emptiest affectation. Well, most men have bound their eyes with one or another handkerchief, and attached themselves to some one of these communities of opinion. This conformity makes them not false in a few particulars, authors of a few lies, but false in all particulars. Their every truth is not quite true. Their two is not the real two, their four not the real four; so that every word they say chagrins us, and we know not where to begin to set them right. Meantime nature is not slow to equip us in the prison-uniform of the party to which we adhere. We come to wear one cut of face and figure, and acquire by degrees the gentlest asinine expression. There is a mortifying experience in particular which does not fail to wreak itself also in the general history; I mean "the foolish face of praise," the forced smile which we put on in company where we do not feel at ease in answer to conversation which does not interest us. The muscles, not spontaneously moved, but moved by a low usurping willfulness, grow tight about the outline of the face with the most disagreeable sensation.

For nonconformity the world whips you with its displeasure. And therefore a man must know how to estimate a sour face. The bystanders look askance on him in the public street or in the friend's parlor. If this aversation had its origin in contempt and resistance like his own, he might well go home with a sad countenance; but the sour faces of the multitude, like their sweet faces, have no deep cause, but are put on and off as the wind blows and a newspaper directs. Yet is the discontent of the multitude more formidable than that of the senate and the college. It is easy enough for a firm man who knows the world to brook the rage of the cultivated classes. Their rage is decorous and prudent, for they are timid as being very vulnerable themselves. But when to their feminine rage the indignation of the people is added, when the ignorant and the poor are aroused, when the unintelligent brute force that lies at the bottom of society is made to growl and mow, it needs the habit of magnanimity and religion to treat it godlike as a trifle of no concernment.

The other terror that scares us from self-trust is our consistency; a reverence for our past act or word, because the eyes of others have no other data for computing our orbit than our past acts, and we are loath to disappoint them.

But why should you keep your head over your shoulder? Why drag about this corpse of your memory, lest you contradict somewhatyou have stated in this or that public place? Suppose you should contradict yourself; what then? It seems to be a rule of wisdom never to rely on your memory alone, scarcely even in acts of pure memory, but to bring the past for judgment into the thousand-eyed present, and live ever in a new day. In your metaphysics you have denied personality to the Deity; yet when the devout motions of the soul come, yield to them heart and life, though they should clothe God with shape and color. Leave your theory, as Joseph his coat in the hand of the harlot, and flee.

A foolish consistency is the hobgoblin of little minds, adored by little statesmen and philosophers and divines. With consistency a great soul has simply nothing to do. He may as well concern himself with the shadow on the wall. Speak what you think now in hard words, and to-morrow speak what to-morrow thinks in hard words again, though it contradict everything you said to-day.—"Ah, so you shall be sure to be misunderstood."—Is it so bad, then, to be misunderstood? Pythagoras was misunderstood, and Socrates, and Jesus, and Luther, and Copernicus, and Galileo, and Newton, and every pure and wise spirit that ever took flesh. To be great is to be misunderstood.

I suppose no man can violate his nature. All the sallies of his will are rounded in by the law of his being, as the inequalities of Andes and Himmaleh are insignificant in the curve of the sphere. Nor does it matter how you gauge and try him. A character is like an acrostic or Alexandrian stanza—read it forward, backward, or across, it still spells the same thing. In this pleasing, contrite wood-life which God allows me, let me record day by day my honest thought without prospect or retrospect, and, I cannot doubt, it will be found symmetrical, though I mean it not, and see it not. My book should smell of pines and resound with the hum of insects. The swallow over my window should interweave that thread or straw he carries in his bill into my web also. We pass for what we are. Character teaches above our wills. Men imagine that they communicate their virtue or vice only by overt actions, and do not see that virtue or vice emit a breath every moment.

There will be an agreement in whatever variety of actions, so they be each honest and natural in their hour. For of one will, the actions will be harmonious, however unlike they seem. These varieties are lost sight of at a little distance, at a little height of thought. One tendency unites them all. The voyage of the best ship is a zigzag line of a hundred tacks. See the line from a sufficient distance, and it straightens itself to the average tendency. Your genuine action will explain itself, and will explain your other genuine actions. Your conformity explains nothing. Act singly, and what you have already done singly will justify you now. Greatness appeals to the future. If I can be firm enough to-day to do right, and scorn eyes, I must have done so much right before as to defend me now. Be it how it will, do right now. Always scorn appearances, and you always may. The force of character is cumulative. All the foregone days of virtue work their health into this. What makes the majesty of the heroes of the senate and the field, which so fills the imagination? The consciousness of a train of great days and victories behind. They shed an united light on the advancing actor. He is attended as by a visible escort of angels. That is it which throws thunder into Chatham's voice, and dignity into Washington's port, and America into Adams's eye. Honor is venerable to us because it is no ephemeris. It is always ancient virtue. We worship it to-day because it is not of to-day. We love it and pay it homage, because it is not a trap for our love and homage, but is self-dependent, self-derived, and therefore of an old immaculate pedigree, even if shown in a young person.

Let a man then know his worth, and keep things under his feet. Let him not peep or steal, or skulk up and down with the air of a charity-boy, a bastard, or an interloper, in the world which exists for him. But the man in the street, finding no worth in himself which corresponds to the force which built a tower or sculptured a marble god, feels poor when he looks on these. To him a palace, a statue, a costly book, have an alien and forbidding air, much like a gay equipage, and seem to say like that, "Who are you, Sir?" Yet they all are his, suitors for his notice, petitioners to his faculties that they will come out and take possession. The picture waits for my verdict: it is not to command me, but I am to settle its claims to praise. That popular fable of the sot who was picked up dead drunk in the street, carried to the duke's house, washed and dressed and laid in the duke's bed, and, on his waking, treated with all obsequious ceremony like the duke, and assured that he had been insane, owes its popularity to the fact that it symbolizes so well the state of man, who is in the world a sort of sot, but now and then wakes up, exercises his reason, and finds himself a true prince.

Man is timid and apologetic; he is no longer upright; he dares not say "I think," "I am," but quotes some saint or sage. He is ashamed before the blade of grass or the blowing rose. These roses under my window make no reference to former roses or to better ones; they are for what they are; they exist with God to-day. There is no time to them. There is simply the rose; it is perfect in every moment of its existence. Before a leaf-bud has burst, its whole life acts; in the full-blown flower there is no more; in the leafless root there is no less. Its nature is satisfied, and it satisfies nature, in all moments alike. But man postpones, or remembers; he does not live in the present, but with a reverted eye laments the past, or, heedless of the riches that surround him, stands on tiptoe to foresee the future. He cannot be happy and strong until he too lives with nature in the present, above time.

It is easy to see that a greater self-reliance must work a revolution in all the offices and relations of men; in their religion; in their education; in their pursuits; their modes of living; their association; in their property; in their speculative views.

1. In what prayers do men allow themselves! That which they call a holy office is not so much as brave and manly. Prayer looks abroad and asks for some foreign addition to come through some foreign virtue, and loses itself in endless mazes of natural and supernatural, and mediatorial and miraculous. Prayer that craves a particular commodity,— anything less than all good,—is vicious. Prayer is the contemplation of the facts of life from the highest point of view. It is the soliloquy of a beholding and jubilant soul. It is the spirit of God pronouncing his works good. But prayer as a means to effect a private end is meanness and theft. It supposes dualism and not unity in nature and consciousness.

As soon as the man is at one with God, he will not beg.

2. It is for want of self-culture that the superstition of Traveling, whose idols are Italy, England, Egypt, retains its fascination for all educated Americans. They who made England, Italy, or Greece venerable in the imagination did so by sticking fast where they were, like an axis of the earth. In manly hours, we feel that duty is our place. The soul is no traveler; the wise man stays at home, and when his necessities, his duties, on any occasion call him from his house, or into foreign lands, he is at home still; and shall make men sensible by the expression of his countenance, that he goes the missionary of wisdom and virtue, and visits cities and men like a sovereign, and not like an interloper or a valet.

3. Traveling is a fool's paradise. Our first journeys discover to us the indifference of places. At home I dream that at Naples, at Rome, I can be intoxicated with beauty, and lose my sadness. I pack my trunk, embrace my friends, embark on the sea, and at last wake up in Naples, and there beside me is the stern fact, the sad self, unrelenting, identical, that I fled from. I seek the Vatican, and the palaces. I affect to be intoxicated with sights and suggestions, but I am

not intoxicated. My giant goes with me wherever I
go.

4. But the rage of traveling is a symptom of a deeper
unsoundness affecting the whole intellectual
action. The intellect is vagabond, and our system
of education fosters restlessness. Our minds travel
when our bodies are forced to stay at home. We
imitate; and what is imitation but the traveling of
the mind? Our houses are built with foreign taste;
our shelves are garnished with foreign ornaments;
our opinions, our tastes, our faculties, lean, and
follow the Past and the Distant. The soul created
the arts wherever they have flourished. It was in
his own mind that the artist sought his model. It
was an application of his own thought to the thing
to be done and the conditions to be observed. And
why need we copy the Doric or the Gothic model?
Beauty, convenience, grandeur of thought, and
quaint expression are as near to us as to any, and
if the American artist will study with hope and love
the precise thing to be done by him considering the
climate, the soil, the length of the day, the wants of
the people, the habit and form of the government,
he will create a house in which all these will find
themselves fitted, and taste and sentiment will be
satisfied also.

5. As our Religion, our Education, our Art look abroad, so does our spirit of society. All men plume themselves on the improvement of society, and no man improves.

Society never advances. It recedes as fast on one side as it gains on the other. It undergoes continual changes; it is barbarous, it is civilized, it is Christianized, it is rich, it is scientific; but this change is not amelioration. For everything that is given, something is taken. Society acquires new arts, and loses old instincts. What a contrast between the well-clad, reading, writing, thinking American, with a watch, a pencil, and a bill of exchange in his pocket, and the naked New Zealander, whose property is a club, a spear, a mat, and an undivided twentieth of a shed to sleep under! But compare the health of the two men, and you shall see that the white man has lost his aboriginal strength. If the traveler tells us truly, strike the savage with a broad ax, and in a day or two the flesh shall unite and heal as if you struck the blow into soft pitch, and the same blow shall send the white to his grave.

The civilized man has built a coach, but has lost the use of his feet. He is supported on crutches, but lacks so much support of muscle. He has a fine Geneva watch, but he fails of the skill to tell the hour by the sun. A Greenwich nautical almanac he has, and so being sure of the information when he wants it, the man in the street does not know a star in the sky. The solstice he does not observe; the equinox he knows as little; and the whole bright calendar of the year is without a dial in his mind. His notebooks impair his memory; his libraries overload his wit; the insurance office increases the number of accidents; and it may be a question whether machinery does not encumber; whether we have not lost by refinement some energy, by a Christianity entrenched in establishments and forms, some vigor of wild virtue. For every Stoic was a Stoic; but in Christendom where is the Christian?

There is no more deviation in the moral standard than in the standard of height or bulk. No greater men are now than ever were. A singular equality may be observed between great men of the first and of the last ages; nor can all the science, art, religion, and philosophy of the nineteenth century avail to educate greater men than Plutarch's heroes, three or four and twenty centuries ago. Not in time is the race progressive. Phocion, Socrates, Anaxagoras, Diogenes, are great men, but they leave no class. He who is really of their class will not be called by their name, but will be his own man, and, in his turn, the founder of a sect. The arts and inventions of each period are only its costume, and do not invigorate men. The harm of the improved machinery may compensate its good. Hudson and Bering accomplished so much in their fishing boats, as to astonish Parry and Franklin, whose equipment exhausted the resources of science and art. Galileo, with an opera-glass, discovered a more splendid series of celestial phenomena than any one since. Columbus found the New World in an undecked boat. It is curious to see the periodical disuse and perishing of means and machinery, which were introduced with loud laudation a few years or centuries before. The great genius returns to essential man. We reckoned the improvements of the art of war among the triumphs of science, and yet Napoleon conquered Europe by the bivouac, which consisted of falling back on naked valor, and disencumbering it of all aids. The Emperor held it impossible to make a perfect army, says Las Casas, "without abolishing our arms, magazines, commissaries, and carriages, until, in imitation of the Roman custom, the soldier should receive his supply of corn, grind it in his handmill, and bake his bread himself."

Society is a wave. The wave moves onward, but the water of which it is composed does not. The same particle does not rise from the valley to the ridge. Its unity is only phenomenal. The persons who make up a nation to-day, next year die, and their experience with them.

And so the reliance on Property, including the reliance on governments which protect it, is the want of self-reliance. Men have looked away from themselves and at things so long, that they have come to esteem the religious, learned, and civil institutions as guards of property, and they deprecate assaults on these, because they feel them to be assaults on property. They measure their esteem of each other by what each has, and not by what each is. But a cultivated man becomes ashamed of his property, out of new respect for his nature. Especially he hates what he has, if he see that it is accidental,—came to him by inheritance, or gift, or crime; then he feels that it is not having; it does not belong to him, has no root in him, and merely lies there, because no revolution or no robber takes it away. But that which a man is, does always by necessity acquire, and what the man acquires is living property, which does not wait the beck of rulers, or mobs, or revolutions, or fire, or storm, or bankruptcies, but perpetually renews itself wherever the man breathes. "Thy lot or portion of life," said the Caliph Ali, "is seeking after thee; therefore be at rest from seeking after it." Our dependence on these foreign goods leads us to our slavish respect for numbers. The political parties meet in numerous conventions; the greater the concourse, and with each new uproar of announcement, The delegation from Essex! The Democrats from New Hampshire! The Whigs of Maine! the young patriot feels himself stronger than before by a new thousand of eyes and arms. In like manner the reformers summon conventions, and vote and resolve in multitude. Not so, O friends! will the god deign to enter and inhabit you, but by a method precisely the reverse. It is only as a man puts off all foreign support, and stands alone, that I see him to be strong and to prevail. He is weaker by every recruit to his banner. Is not a man better than a town? Ask nothing of men, and in the endless mutation, thou only firm column must presently appear the upholder of all that surrounds thee. He who knows that power is inborn, that he is weak because he has looked for good out of him and elsewhere, and so perceiving, throws himself unhesitatingly on his thought, instantly rights himself, stands in the erect position, commands his limbs, works miracles; just as a man who stands on his feet is stronger than a man who stands on his head.

So use all that is called Fortune. Most men gamble with her, and gain all, and lose all, as her wheel rolls. But do thou leave as unlawful these winnings, and deal with Cause and Effect, the chancelors of God. In the Will work and acquire, and thou hast chained the wheel of Chance, and shalt sit hereafter out of fear from her rotations. A political victory, a rise of rents, the recovery of your sick, or the return of your absent friend, or some other favorable event, raises your spirits, and you think good days are preparing for you. Do not believe it. Nothing can bring you peace but yourself. Nothing can bring you peace but the triumph of principles.

- Do not go where the path may lead, go instead where there is no path and leave a trail.
- To be yourself in a world that is constantly trying to make you something else is the greatest accomplishment.
- People do not seem to realize that their opinion of the world is also a confession of their character.
- The only person you are destined to become is the person you decide to be.
- What you do speaks so loudly that I cannot hear what you say.

EIGHT

How to Remain Motivated in a Demotivating World

Florence Scovell Shinn answers from *The Game of Life and How to Play It*

Florence Scovell Shinn (1871-1940) was an American artist and book illustrator who became a New Thought spiritual teacher and metaphysical writer in her middle years. In New Thought circles, she is best known for her first book, The Game of Life and How to Play It.

Most people consider life a battle, but it is not a battle, it is a game. It is a game, however, which cannot be played successfully without the knowledge of spiritual law, and the Old and the New

Testaments give the rules of the game with wonderful clearness. Jesus Christ taught that it was a great game of Giving and Receiving. "Whatsoever a man soweth that shall he also reap." This means that whatever man sends out in word or deed, will return to him; what he gives, he will receive.

If he gives hate, he will receive hate; if he gives love, he will receive love; if he gives criticism, he will receive criticism; if he lies he will be lied to; if he cheats he will be cheated. We are taught also, that the imaging faculty plays a leading part in the game of life. "Keep thy heart (or imagination) with all diligence, for out of it are the issues of life." (Prov. 4:23.)

This means that what man images, sooner or later externalizes in his affairs, I know of a man who feared a certain disease. It was a very rare disease and difficult to get, but he pictured it continually and read about it until it manifested in his body, and he died, the victim of distorted imagination.

So we see, to play successfully the game of life, we must train the imaging faculty. A person with an imaging faculty trained to image only good, brings into his life "every righteous desire of his heart" - health, wealth, love, friends, perfect self-expression, his highest ideals. The imagination has been called, "The Scissors of The Mind, " and it is ever cutting, cutting, day by day, the pictures man sees there, and sooner or later he meets his own creations in his outer world. To train the imagination successfully, man must understand the workings of his mind. The Greeks said: "Know Thyself."

There are three departments of the mind, the subconscious, conscious and superconscious. The subconscious, is simply power, without direction. It is like steam or electricity, and it does what it is directed to do; it has no power of induction. Whatever man feels deeply or images clearly, is impressed upon the subconscious mind, and carried out in minutest detail.

For example: a woman I know, when a child, always "made believe" she was a widow. She "dressed up" in black clothes and wore a long black veil, and people thought she was very clever and amusing. She grew up and married a man with whom she was deeply in love. In a short time he died and she wore black and a sweeping veil for many years. The picture of herself as a widow was impressed upon the subconscious mind, and in due time worked itself out, regardless of the havoc created.

The conscious mind has been called mortal or carnal mind. It is the human mind and sees life as it appears to be. It sees death, disaster, sickness, poverty and limitation of every kind, and it impresses the subconscious. The superconscious mind is the God Mind within each man, and is the realm of perfect ideas. In it, is the "perfect pattern" spoken of by Plato, The Divine Design; for there is a Divine Design for each person.

"There is a place that you are to fill and no one else can fill, something you are to do, which no one else can do." There is a perfect picture of this in the superconscious mind. It usually flashes across the conscious as an unattainable ideal - "something too good to be true." In reality it is man's true destiny (or destination) flashed to him from the Infinite Intelligence which is within himself. Many people, however, are in ignorance of their true destinies and are striving for things and situations which do not belong to them, and would only bring failure and dissatisfaction if attained.

For example: A woman came to me and asked me to "speak the word" that she would marry a certain man with whom she was very much in love. (She called him A. B.) I replied that this would be a violation of spiritual law, but that I would speak the word for the right man, the "divine selection, " the man who belonged to her by divine right.

I added, "If A. B. is the right man you can't lose him, and if he isn't, you will receive his equivalent." She saw A. B. frequently but no headway was made in their friendship. One evening she called, and said, "Do you know, for the last week, A. B. hasn't seemed so wonderful to me." I replied, "Maybe he is not the divine selection - another man my be the right one." Soon after that, she met another man who fell in love with her at once, and who said she was his ideal.

In fact, he said all the things that she had always wished A. B. would say to her. She remarked, "It was quite uncanny." She soon returned his love, and lost all interest in A. B.

This shows the law of substitution. A right idea was substituted for a wrong one, therefore there was no loss or sacrifice involved. Jesus Christ said, "Seek ye first the kingdom of God and his righteousness; and all these things shall be added unto you, " and he said the Kingdom was within man. The Kingdom is the realm of right ideas, or the divine pattern. Jesus Christ taught that man's words played a leading part in the game of life. "By your words ye are justified and by your words ye are condemned."

Many people have brought disaster into their lives through idle words. For example: A woman once asked me why her life was now one of poverty of limitation. Formerly she had a home, was surrounded by beautiful things and had often tired of the management of her home, and had said repeatedly, "I'm sick and tired of things - I wish I lived in a trunk, " and she added: "Today I am living in that trunk." She had spoken herself into a trunk. The subconscious mind has no sense of humor and people often joke themselves into unhappy experiences. For example: A woman who had a great deal of money, joked continually about "getting ready for the poorhouse."

In a few years she was almost destitute, having impressed the subconscious mind with a picture of lack and limitation. Fortunately the law works both ways, and a situation of lack may be changed to one of plenty. For example: A woman came to me one hot summer's day for a "treatment" for prosperity. She was worn out, dejected and discouraged. She said she possessed just eight dollars in the world. I said, "Good, we'll bless the eight dollars and multiply them as Jesus Christ multiplied the loaves and fishes, " for He taught that every man had the power to bless and to multiply, to heal and to prosper. She said, "What shall I do next?"

I replied, "Follow intuition. Have you a 'hunch' to do anything, or to go anywhere?" Intuition means, intuition, or to be taught from within. It is man's unerring guide, and I will deal more fully with its laws in a following chapter. The woman replied: "I don't know - I seem to have a 'hunch' to go home; I've just enough money for carfare." Her home was in a distant city and was one of lack and limitation, and the reasoning mind (or intellect) would have said: "Stay in New York and get work and make some money." I replied, "Then go home—never violate a hunch." I spoke the following words for her: Infinite Spirit open the way for great abundance for—. She is an irresistible magnet for all that belongs to her by divine right." I told her to repeat it continually also. She left for home immediately. In calling on a woman one day, she linked up with an old friend of her family.

Through this friend, she received thousands of dollars in a most miraculous way. She has said to me often, "Tell people about the woman who came to you with eight dollars and a hunch." There is always plenty on man's pathway; but it can only be brought into manifestation through desire, faith or the spoken word. Jesus Christ brought out clearly that man must make the first move. "Ask, and it shall be given you, seek, and ye shall find, knock, and it shall be opened unto you. (Mat. 7:7). In the scriptures we read:

"Concerning the works of my hands, command ye me." Infinite Intelligence, God, is ever ready to carry out man's smallest or greatest demands. Every desire, uttered or unexpressed, is a demand. We are often startled by having a wish suddenly fulfilled. For example: One Easter, having seen many beautiful rosetrees in the florists' windows, I wished I would receive one, and for an instant saw it mentally being carried in the door. Easter came, and with it a beautiful rose-tree. I thanked my friend the following day, and told her it was just what I had wanted. She replied, "I didn't send you a rose-tree, I sent you lilies!" "The man had mixed the order, and sent me a rose-tree simply because I had started the law in action, and I had to have a rose-tree.

Nothing stands between man and his highest ideals and every desire of his heart, but doubt and fear. When man can "wish without worrying, " every desire will be instantly fulfilled. I will explain more fully in a following chapter the scientific reason for this and fear must be erased from the consciousness. It is man's only enemy - fear of lack, fear of failure, fear of sickness, fear of loss and a feeling of insecurity on some plane. Jesus Christ said: "Why are ye fearful, oh ye of little faith?" (Mat. 8:26) So we can see we must substitute faith for fear, for fear is only inverted faith; it is faith in evil instead of good. The object of the game of life is to see clearly one's good and to obliterate all mental pictures of evil. This must be done by impressing the subconscious mind with a realization of good. A very brilliant man, who has attained great success, told me he had suddenly erased all fear from his consciousness by reading a sign which hung in a room. He saw printed, in large letters this statement - Why worry, it will probably never happen." These words were stamped indelibly upon his subconscious mind, and he has now a firm conviction that only good can come into his life, therefore only good can manifest.

Every thought, every word is impressed upon it and carried out in amazing detail. It is like a singer making a record on the sensitive disc of the phonographic plate. Every note and tone of the singer's voice is registered. If he coughs or hesitates, it is registered also. So let us break all the old bad records in the subconscious mind, the records of our lives which we do not wish to keep, and make new and beautiful ones. Speak these words aloud, with power and conviction: "I now smash and demolish (by my spoken word) every untrue record in my subconscious mind. They shall return to the dust-heap of their native nothingness, for they came from my own vain imaginings. I now make my perfect records through the Christ within - The records of Health, Wealth, Love and perfect self-Expression." This is the square of life, The Game completed.

- You will be a failure, until you impress the subconscious with the conviction you are a success. This is done by making an affirmation which clicks.
- If one asks for success and prepares for failure, he will get the situation he has prepared for.
- There is a place that you are to fill, something you are to do, which no one else can do.
- The simple rules are fearless faith, nonresistance and love.
- No man is a success in business unless he loves his work.

NINE

How to Increase Your Willpower and Achieve Amazing Results

Samuel Smiles answers from *Self-Help*

Samuel Smiles (1812-1904) was a Scot who originally trained as a doctor before turning to journalism full-time. Smiles wrote for a popular audience to show people how best to take advantage of the changes being brought about by the industrial revolution which was sweeping Britain and other parts of the world in the first half of the 19th century. In his best known work, Self-Help, *he combines Victorian morality with sound free market ideas into moral tales showing the benefits of thrift, hard work, education, perseverance, and a sound moral character.*

"This above all,—To thine own self be true;
And it must follow, as the night the day,
Then canst not then be false to any man."

National and Individual:
Heaven helps those who help themselves" is a well-tried maxim, embodying in a small compass the results of vast human experience. The spirit of self-help is the root of all genuine growth in the individual; and, exhibited in the lives of many, it constitutes the true source of national vigour and strength. Help from without is often enfeebling in its effects, but help from within invariably invigorates. Whatever is done for men or classes, to a certain extent takes away the stimulus and necessity of doing for themselves; and where men are subjected to over-guidance and over-government, the inevitable tendency is to render them comparatively helpless.

Even the best institutions can give a man no active help. Perhaps the most they can do is, to leave him free to develop himself and improve his individual condition. But in all times men have been prone to believe that their happiness and well-being were to be secured by means of institutions rather than by their own conduct. Hence the value of legislation as an agent in human advancement has usually been much over-estimated. To constitute the millionth part of a Legislature, by voting for one or two men once in three or five years, however conscientiously this duty may be performed, can exercise but little active influence upon any man's life and character. Moreover, it is every day becoming more clearly understood, that the function of Government is negative and restrictive, rather than positive and active; being resolvable principally into protection—protection of life, liberty, and property. Laws, wisely administered, will secure men in the enjoyment of the fruits of their labour, whether of mind or body, at a comparatively small personal sacrifice; but no laws, however stringent, can make the idle industrious, the thriftless provident, or the drunken sober. Such reforms can only be effected by means of individual action, economy, and self-denial; by better habits, rather than by greater rights.

The Government of a nation itself is usually found to be but the reflex of the individuals composing it. The Government that is ahead of the people will inevitably be dragged down to their level, as the Government that is behind them will in the long run be dragged up. In the order of nature, the collective character of a nation will as surely find its befitting results in its law and government, as water finds its own level. The noble people will be nobly ruled, and the ignorant and corrupt ignobly. Indeed all experience serves to prove that the worth and strength of a State depend far less upon the form of its institutions than upon the character of its men. For the nation is only an aggregate of individual conditions, and civilization itself is but a question of the personal improvement of the men, women, and children of whom society is composed.

National progress is the sum of individual industry, energy, and uprightness, as national decay is of individual idleness, selfishness, and vice. What we are accustomed to decry as great social evils, will, for the most part, be found to be but the outgrowth of man's own perverted life; and though we may endeavour to cut them down and extirpate them by means of Law, they will only spring up again with fresh luxuriance in some other form, unless the conditions of personal life and character are radically improved. If this view be correct, then it follows that the highest patriotism and philanthropy consist, not so much in altering laws and modifying institutions, as in helping and stimulating men to elevate and improve themselves by their own free and independent individual action.

It may be of comparatively little consequence how a man is governed from without, whilst everything depends upon how he governs himself from within. The greatest slave is not he who is ruled by a despot, great though that evil be, but he who is the thrall of his own moral ignorance, selfishness, and vice. Nations who are thus enslaved at heart cannot be freed by any mere changes of masters or of institutions; and so long as the fatal delusion prevails, that liberty solely depends upon and consists in government, so long will such changes, no matter at what cost they may be effected, have as little practical and lasting result as the shifting of the figures in a phantasmagoria. The solid foundations of liberty must rest upon individual character; which is also the only sure guarantee for social security and national progress. John Stuart Mill truly observes that "even despotism does not produce its worst effects so long as individuality exists under it; and whatever crushes individuality is despotism, by whatever name it be called."

Old fallacies as to human progress are constantly turning up. Some call for Cæsars, others for Nationalities, and others for Acts of Parliament. We are to wait for Cæsars, and when they are found, "happy the people who recognise and follow them." [4] This doctrine shortly means, everything for the people, nothing by them,—a doctrine which, if taken as a guide, must, by destroying the free conscience of a community, speedily prepare the way for any form of despotism. Cæsarism is human idolatry in its worst form—a worship of mere power, as degrading in its effects as the worship of mere wealth would be. A far healthier doctrine to inculcate among the nations would be that of Self-Help; and so soon as it is thoroughly understood and carried into action, Cæsarism will be no more. The two principles are directly antagonistic; and what Victor Hugo said of the Pen and the Sword alike applies to them, "Ceci tuera cela." [This will kill that.]

The power of Nationalities and Acts of Parliament is also a prevalent superstition. What William Dargan, one of Ireland's truest patriots, said at the closing of the first Dublin Industrial Exhibition, may well be quoted now. "To tell the truth," he said, "I never heard the word independence mentioned that my own country and my own fellow townsmen did not occur to my mind. I have heard a great deal about the independence that we were to get from this, that, and the other place, and of the great expectations we were to have from persons from other countries coming amongst us. Whilst I value as much as any man the great advantages that must result to us from that intercourse, I have always been deeply impressed with the feeling that our industrial independence is dependent upon ourselves. I believe that with simple industry and careful exactness in the utilization of our energies, we never had a fairer chance nor a brighter prospect than the present. We have made a step, but perseverance is the great agent of success; and if we but go on zealously, I believe in my conscience that in a short period we shall arrive at a position of equal comfort, of equal happiness, and of equal independence, with that of any other people."

All nations have been made what they are by the thinking

and the working of many generations of men. Patient and persevering labourers in all ranks and conditions of life, cultivators of the soil and explorers of the mine, inventors and discoverers, manufacturers, mechanics and artisans, poets, philosophers, and politicians, all have contributed towards the grand result, one generation building upon another's labours, and carrying them forward to still higher stages. This constant succession of noble workers—the artisans of civilisation—has served to create order out of chaos in industry, science, and art; and the living race has thus, in the course of nature, become the inheritor of the rich estate provided by the skill and industry of our forefathers, which is placed in our hands to cultivate, and to hand down, not only unimpaired but improved, to our successors.

The spirit of self-help, as exhibited in the energetic action of individuals, has in all times been a marked feature in the English character, and furnishes the true measure of our power as a nation. Rising above the heads of the mass, there were always to be found a series of individuals distinguished beyond others, who commanded the public homage. But our progress has also been owing to multitudes of smaller and less known men. Though only the generals' names may be remembered in the history of any great campaign, it has been in a great measure through the individual valour and heroism of the privates that victories have been won. And life, too, is "a soldiers' battle,"—men in the ranks having in all times been amongst the greatest of workers. Many are the lives of men unwritten, which have nevertheless as powerfully influenced civilisation and progress as the more fortunate Great whose names are recorded in biography. Even the humblest person, who sets before his fellows an example of industry, sobriety, and upright honesty of purpose in life, has a present as well as a future influence upon the well-being of his country; for his life and character pass unconsciously into the lives of others, and propagate good example for all time to come.

Daily experience shows that it is energetic individualism which produces the most powerful effects upon the life and action of others, and really constitutes the best practical education. Schools, academies, and colleges, give but the merest beginnings of culture in comparison with it. Far more influential is the life-education daily given in our homes, in the streets, behind counters, in workshops, at the loom and the plough, in counting-houses and manufactories, and in the busy haunts of men. This is that finishing instruction as members of society, which Schiller designated "the education of the human race," consisting in action, conduct, self-culture, self-control,—all that tends to discipline a man truly, and fit him for the proper performance of the duties and business of life,—a kind of education not to be learnt from books, or acquired by any amount of mere literary training. With his usual weight of words Bacon observes, that "Studies teach not their own use; but that is a wisdom without them, and above them, won by observation;" a remark that holds true of actual life, as well as of the cultivation of the intellect itself. For all experience serves to illustrate and enforce the lesson, that a man perfects himself by work more than by reading,—that it is life rather than literature, action rather than study, and character rather than biography, which tend perpetually to renovate mankind.

Biographies of great, but especially of good men, are nevertheless most instructive and useful, as helps, guides, and incentives to others. Some of the best are almost equivalent to gospels—teaching high living, high thinking, and energetic action for their own and the world's good. The valuable examples which they furnish of the power of self-help, of patient purpose, resolute working, and steadfast integrity, issuing in the formation of truly noble and manly character, exhibit in language not to be misunderstood, what it is in the power of each to accomplish for himself; and eloquently illustrate the efficacy of self-respect and self-reliance in enabling men of even the humblest rank to work out for themselves an honourable competency and a solid reputation.

Great men of science, literature, and art—apostles of great thoughts and lords of the great heart—have belonged to no exclusive class nor rank in life. They have come alike from colleges, workshops, and farmhouses,—from the huts of poor men and the mansions of the rich. Some of God's greatest apostles have come from "the ranks." The poorest have sometimes taken the highest places; nor have difficulties apparently the most insuperable proved obstacles in their way. Those very difficulties, in many instances, would ever seem to have been their best helpers, by evoking their powers of labour and endurance, and stimulating into life faculties which might otherwise have lain dormant. The instances of obstacles thus surmounted, and of triumphs thus achieved, are indeed so numerous, as almost to justify the proverb that "with Will one can do anything." Take, for instance, the remarkable fact, that from the barber's shop came Jeremy Taylor, the most poetical of divines; Sir Richard Arkwright, the inventor of the spinning-jenny and founder of the cotton manufacture; Lord Tenterden, one of the most distinguished of Lord Chief Justices; and Turner, the greatest among landscape painters.

No one knows to a certainty what Shakespeare was; but it is unquestionable that he sprang from a humble rank. His father was a butcher and grazier; and Shakespeare himself is supposed to have been in early life a woolcomber; whilst others aver that he was an usher in a school and afterwards a scrivener's clerk. He truly seems to have been "not one, but all mankind's epitome." For such is the accuracy of his sea phrases that a naval writer alleges that he must have been a sailor; whilst a clergyman infers, from internal evidence in his writings, that he was probably a parson's clerk; and a distinguished judge of horse-flesh insists that he must have been a horse-dealer. Shakespeare was certainly an actor, and in the course of his life "played many parts," gathering his wonderful stores of knowledge from a wide field of experience and observation. In any event, he must have been a close student and a hard worker; and to this day his writings continue to exercise a powerful influence on the formation of English character.

The common class of day labourers has given us Brindley the engineer, Cook the navigator, and Burns the poet. Masons and bricklayers can boast of Ben Jonson, who worked at the building of Lincoln's Inn, with a trowel in his hand and a book in his pocket, Edwards and Telford the engineers, Hugh Miller the geologist, and Allan Cunningham the writer and sculptor; whilst among distinguished carpenters we find the names of Inigo Jones the architect, Harrison the chronometer-maker, John Hunter the physiologist, Romney and Opie the painters, Professor Lee the Orientalist, and John Gibson the sculptor.

From the weaver class have sprung Simson the mathematician, Bacon the sculptor, the two Milners, Adam Walker, John Foster, Wilson the ornithologist, Dr. Livingstone the missionary traveller, and Tannahill the poet.

Shoemakers have given us Sir Cloudesley Shovel the great Admiral, Sturgeon the electrician, Samuel Drew the essayist, Gifford the editor of the 'Quarterly Review,' Bloomfield the poet, and William Carey the missionary; whilst Morrison, another laborious missionary, was a maker of shoe-lasts. Within the last few years, a profound naturalist has been discovered in the person of a shoemaker at Banff, named Thomas Edwards, who, while maintaining himself by his trade, has devoted his leisure to the study of natural science in all its branches, his researches in connexion with the smaller crustaceæ having been rewarded by the discovery of a new species, to which the name of "Praniza Edwardsii" has been given by naturalists.

Nor have tailors been undistinguished. John Stow, the historian, worked at the trade during some part of his life. Jackson, the painter, made clothes until he reached manhood. The brave Sir John Hawkswood, who so greatly distinguished himself at Poictiers, and was knighted by Edward III. for his valour, was in early life apprenticed to a London tailor. Admiral Hobson, who broke the boom at Vigo in 1702, belonged to the same calling. He was working as a tailor's apprentice near Bonchurch, in the Isle of Wight, when the news flew through the village that a squadron of men-of-war was sailing off the island. He sprang from the shopboard, and ran down with his comrades to the beach, to gaze upon the glorious sight.

The boy was suddenly inflamed with the ambition to be a sailor; and springing into a boat, he rowed off to the squadron, gained the admiral's ship, and was accepted as a volunteer. Years after, he returned to his native village full of honours, and dined off bacon and eggs in the cottage where he had worked as an apprentice. But the greatest tailor of all is unquestionably Andrew Johnson, the present President of the United States—a man of extraordinary force of character and vigour of intellect. In his great speech at Washington, when describing himself as having begun his political career as an alderman, and run through all the branches of the legislature, a voice in the crowd cried, "From a tailor up." It was characteristic of Johnson to take the intended sarcasm in good part, and even to turn it to account. "Some gentleman says I have been a tailor. That does not disconcert me in the least; for when I was a tailor I had the reputation of being a good one, and making close fits; I was always punctual with my customers, and always did good work."

The instances of men, in this and other countries, who, by dint of persevering application and energy, have raised themselves from the humblest ranks of industry to eminent positions of usefulness and influence in society, are indeed so numerous that they have long ceased to be regarded as exceptional. Looking at some of the more remarkable, it might almost be said that early encounter with difficulty and adverse circumstances was the necessary and indispensable condition of success. The British House of Commons has always contained a considerable number of such self-raised men—fitting representatives of the industrial character of the people; and it is to the credit of our Legislature that they have been welcomed and honoured there. When the late Joseph Brotherton, member for Salford, in the course of the discussion on the Ten Hours Bill, detailed with true pathos the hardships and fatigues to which he had been subjected when working as a factory boy in a cotton mill, and described the resolution which he had then formed, that if ever it was in his power he would endeavour to ameliorate the condition of that class, Sir James Graham rose immediately after him, and declared, amidst the cheers of the House, that he did not before know that Mr. Brotherton's origin had been so humble, but that it rendered him more proud than he had ever before been of the House of Commons, to think that a person risen from that condition should be able to sit side by side, on equal terms, with the hereditary gentry of the land.

LEADERS OF INDUSTRY—INVENTORS AND PRODUCERS

One of the most strongly-marked features of the English people is their spirit of industry, standing out prominent and distinct in their past history, and as strikingly characteristic of them now as at any former period. It is this spirit, displayed by the commons of England, which has laid the foundations and built up the industrial greatness of the empire. This vigorous growth of the nation has been mainly the result of the free energy of individuals, and it has been contingent upon the number of hands and minds from time to time actively employed within it, whether as cultivators of the soil, producers of articles of utility, contrivers of tools and machines, writers of books, or creators of works of art. And while this spirit of active industry has been the vital principle of the nation, it has also been its saving and remedial one, counteracting from time to time the effects of errors in our laws and imperfections in our constitution.

The career of industry which the nation has pursued, has also proved its best education. As steady application to work is the healthiest training for every individual, so is it the best discipline of a state. Honourable industry travels the same road with duty; and Providence has closely linked both with happiness. The gods, says the poet, have placed labour and toil on the way leading to the Elysian fields. Certain it is that no bread eaten by man is so sweet as that earned by his own labour, whether bodily or mental. By labour the earth has been subdued, and man redeemed from barbarism; nor has a single step in civilization been made without it. Labour is not only a necessity and a duty, but a blessing: only the idler feels it to be a curse. The duty of work is written on the thews and muscles of the limbs, the mechanism of the hand, the nerves and lobes of the brain—the sum of whose healthy action is satisfaction and enjoyment. In the school of labour is taught the best practical wisdom; nor is a life of manual employment, as we shall hereafter find, incompatible with high mental culture.

Hugh Miller, than whom none knew better the strength and the weakness belonging to the lot of labour, stated the result of his experience to be, that Work, even the hardest, is full of pleasure and materials for self-improvement. He held honest labour to be the best of teachers, and that the school of toil is the noblest of schools—save only the Christian one—that it is a school in which the ability of being useful is imparted, the spirit of independence learnt, and the habit of persevering effort acquired. He was even of opinion that the training of the mechanic—by the exercise which it gives to his observant faculties, from his daily dealing with things actual and practical, and the close experience of life which he acquires—better fits him for picking his way along the journey of life, and is more favourable to his growth as a Man, emphatically speaking, than the training afforded by any other condition.

Inventors have set in motion some of the greatest industries of the world. To them society owes many of its chief necessaries, comforts, and luxuries; and by their genius and labour daily life has been rendered in all respects more easy as well as enjoyable. Our food, our clothing, the furniture of our homes, the glass which admits the light to our dwellings at the same time that it excludes the cold, the gas which illuminates our streets, our means of locomotion by land and by sea, the tools by which our various articles of necessity and luxury are fabricated, have been the result of the labour and ingenuity of many men and many minds. Mankind at large are all the happier for such inventions, and are every day reaping the benefit of them in an increase of individual well-being as well as of public enjoyment.

Though the invention of the working steam-engine— the king of machines—belongs, comparatively speaking, to our own epoch, the idea of it was born many centuries ago. Like other contrivances and discoveries, it was effected step by step—one man transmitting the result of his labours, at the time apparently useless, to his successors, who took it up and carried it forward another stage—the prosecution of the inquiry extending over many generations. Thus the idea promulgated by Hero of Alexandria was never altogether lost; but, like the grain of wheat hid in the hand of the Egyptian mummy, it sprouted and again grew vigorously when brought into the full light of modern science. The steam-engine was nothing, however, until it emerged from the state of theory, and was taken in hand by practical mechanics; and what a noble story of patient, laborious investigation, of difficulties encountered and overcome by heroic industry, does not that marvellous machine tell of! It is indeed, in itself, a monument of the power of self-help in man. Grouped around it we find Savary, the military engineer; Newcomen, the Dartmouth blacksmith; Cawley, the glazier; Potter, the engine-boy; Smeaton, the civil engineer; and, towering above all, the laborious, patient, never-tiring James Watt, the mathematical-instrument maker.

It is at the price of lives such as these that the wonders of civilisation are achieved.

APPLICATION AND PERSEVERANCE

THE greatest results in life are usually attained by simple means, and the exercise of ordinary qualities. The common life of every day, with its cares, necessities, and duties, affords ample opportunity for acquiring experience of the best kind; and its most beaten paths provide the true worker with abundant scope for effort and room for self-improvement. The road of human welfare lies along the old highway of steadfast well-doing; and they who are the most persistent, and work in the truest spirit, will usually be the most successful.

Fortune has often been blamed for her blindness; but fortune is not so blind as men are. Those who look into practical life will find that fortune is usually on the side of the industrious, as the winds and waves are on the side of the best navigators. In the pursuit of even the highest branches of human inquiry, the commoner qualities are found the most useful—such as common sense, attention, application, and perseverance. Genius may not be necessary, though even genius of the highest sort does not disdain the use of these ordinary qualities. The very greatest men have been among the least believers in the power of genius, and as worldly wise and persevering as successful men of the commoner sort. Some have even defined genius to be only common sense intensified. A distinguished teacher and president of a college spoke of it as the power of making efforts. John Foster held it to be the power of lighting one's own fire. Buffon said of genius "it is patience."

Newton's was unquestionably a mind of the very highest order, and yet, when asked by what means he had worked out his extraordinary discoveries, he modestly answered, "By always thinking unto them." At another time he thus expressed his method of study: "I keep the subject continually before me, and wait till the first dawnings open slowly by little and little into a full and clear light." It was in Newton's case, as in every other, only by diligent application and perseverance that his great reputation was achieved. Even his recreation consisted in change of study, laying down one subject to take up another. To Dr. Bentley he said: "If I have done the public any service, it is due to nothing but industry and patient thought." So Kepler, another great philosopher, speaking of his studies and his progress, said: "As in Virgil, 'Fama mobilitate viget, vires acquirit eundo,' so it was with me, that the diligent thought on these things was the occasion of still further thinking; until at last I brooded with the whole energy of my mind upon the subject."

The extraordinary results effected by dint of sheer industry and perseverance, have led many distinguished men to doubt whether the gift of genius be so exceptional an endowment as it is usually supposed to be. Thus Voltaire held that it is only a very slight line of separation that divides the man of genius from the man of ordinary mould. Beccaria was even of opinion that all men might be poets and orators, and Reynolds that they might be painters and sculptors. If this were really so, that stolid Englishman might not have been so very far wrong after all, who, on Canova's death, inquired of his brother whether it was "his intention to carry on the business!" Locke, Helvetius, and Diderot believed that all men have an equal aptitude for genius, and that what some are able to effect, under the laws which regulate the operations of the intellect, must also be within the reach of others who, under like circumstances, apply themselves to like pursuits. But while admitting to the fullest extent the wonderful achievements of labour, and recognising the fact that men of the most distinguished genius have invariably been found the most indefatigable workers, it must nevertheless be sufficiently obvious that, without the original endowment of heart and brain, no amount of labour, however well applied, could have produced a Shakespeare, a Newton, a Beethoven, or a Michael Angelo.

Dalton, the chemist, repudiated the notion of his being "a genius," attributing everything which he had accomplished to simple industry and accumulation. John Hunter said of himself, "My mind is like a beehive; but full as it is of buzz and apparent confusion, it is yet full of order and regularity, and food collected with incessant industry from the choicest stores of nature." We have, indeed, but to glance at the biographies of great men to find that the most distinguished inventors, artists, thinkers, and workers of all kinds, owe their success, in a great measure, to their indefatigable industry and application. They were men who turned all things to gold—even time itself. Disraeli the elder held that the secret of success consisted in being master of your subject, such mastery being attainable only through continuous application and study. Hence it happens that the men who have most moved the world, have not been so much men of genius, strictly so called, as men of intense mediocre abilities, and untiring perseverance; not so often the gifted, of naturally bright and shining qualities, as those who have applied themselves diligently to their work, in whatsoever line that might lie. "Alas!" said a widow, speaking of her brilliant but careless son, "he has not the gift of continuance." Wanting in perseverance, such volatile natures are outstripped in the race of life by the diligent and even the dull. "Che va piano, va longano, e va lontano," says the Italian proverb: Who goes slowly, goes long, and goes far.

Progress, however, of the best kind, is comparatively slow. Great results cannot be achieved at once; and we must be satisfied to advance in life as we walk, step by step. De Maistre says that "to know *how to wait* is the great secret of success." We must sow before we can reap, and often have to wait long, content meanwhile to look patiently forward in hope; the fruit best worth waiting for often ripening the slowest. But "time and patience," says the Eastern proverb, "change the mulberry leaf to satin."

To wait patiently, however, men must work cheerfully. Cheerfulness is an excellent working quality, imparting great elasticity to the character. As a bishop has said, "Temper is nine-tenths of Christianity;" so are cheerfulness and diligence nine-tenths of practical wisdom. They are the life and soul of success, as well as of happiness; perhaps the very highest pleasure in life consisting in clear, brisk, conscious working; energy, confidence, and every other good quality mainly depending upon it. Sydney Smith, when labouring as a parish priest at Foston-le-Clay, in Yorkshire,—though he did not feel himself to be in his proper element,—went cheerfully to work in the firm determination to do his best. "I am resolved," he said, "to like it, and reconcile myself to it, which is more manly than to feign myself above it, and to send up complaints by the post of being thrown away, and being desolate, and such like trash." So Dr. Hook, when leaving Leeds for a new sphere of labour said, "Wherever I may be, I shall, by God's blessing, do with my might what my hand findeth to do; and if I do not find work, I shall make it."

Labourers for the public good especially, have to work long and patiently, often uncheered by the prospect of immediate recompense or result. The seeds they sow sometimes lie hidden under the winter's snow, and before the spring comes the husbandman may have gone to his rest. It is not every public worker who, like Rowland Hill, sees his great idea bring forth fruit in his life-time. Adam Smith sowed the seeds of a great social amelioration in that dingy old University of Glasgow where he so long laboured, and laid the foundations of his 'Wealth of Nations;' but seventy years passed before his work bore substantial fruits, nor indeed are they all gathered in yet.

Nothing can compensate for the loss of hope in a man: it entirely changes the character. "How can I work— how can I be happy," said a great but miserable thinker, "when I have lost all hope?" One of the most cheerful and courageous, because one of the most hopeful of workers, was Carey, the missionary. When in India, it was no uncommon thing for him to weary out three pundits, who officiated as his clerks, in one day, he himself taking rest only in change of employment. Carey, the son of a shoe-maker, was supported in his labours by Ward, the son of a carpenter, and Marsham, the son of a weaver. By their labours, a magnificent college was erected at Serampore; sixteen flourishing stations were established; the Bible was translated into sixteen languages, and the seeds were sown of a beneficent moral revolution in British India. Carey was never ashamed of the humbleness of his origin. On one occasion, when at the Governor-General's table he over-heard an officer opposite him asking another, loud enough to be heard, whether Carey had not once been a shoemaker: "No, sir," exclaimed Carey immediately; "only a cobbler." An eminently characteristic anecdote has been told of his perseverance as a boy. When climbing a tree one day, his foot slipped, and he fell to the ground, breaking his leg by the fall. He was confined to his bed for weeks, but when he recovered and was able to walk without support, the very first thing he did was to go and climb that tree. Carey had need of this sort of dauntless courage for the great missionary work of his life, and nobly and resolutely he did it.

It was a maxim of Dr. Young, the philosopher, that "Any man can do what any other man has done;" and it is unquestionable that he himself never recoiled from any trials to which he determined to subject himself. It is related of him, that the first time he mounted a horse, he was in company with the grandson of Mr. Barclay of Ury, the well-known sportsman; when the horseman who preceded them leapt a high fence. Young wished to imitate him, but fell off his horse in the attempt. Without saying a word, he remounted, made a second effort, and was again unsuccessful, but this time he was not thrown further than on to the horse's neck, to which he clung. At the third trial, he succeeded, and cleared the fence.

The story of Timour the Tartar learning a lesson of perseverance under adversity from the spider is well known. Not less interesting is the anecdote of Audubon, the American ornithologist, as related by himself: "An accident," he says, "which happened to two hundred of my original drawings, nearly put a stop to my researches in ornithology. I shall relate it, merely to show how far enthusiasm—for by no other name can I call my perseverance—may enable the preserver of nature to surmount the most disheartening difficulties. I left the village of Henderson, in Kentucky, situated on the banks of the Ohio, where I resided for several years, to proceed to Philadelphia on business. I looked to my drawings before my departure, placed them carefully in a wooden box, and gave them in charge of a relative, with injunctions to see that no injury should happen to them. My absence was of several months; and when I returned, after having enjoyed the pleasures of home for a few days, I inquired after my box, and what I was pleased to call my treasure. The box was produced and opened; but reader, feel for me—a pair of Norway rats had taken possession of the whole, and reared a young family among the gnawed bits of paper, which, but a month previous, represented nearly a thousand inhabitants of air! The burning beat which instantly rushed through my brain was too great to be endured without affecting my whole nervous system. I slept for several nights, and the days passed like days of oblivion—until the animal powers being recalled into action through the strength of my constitution, I took up my gun, my notebook, and my pencils, and went forth to the woods as gaily as if nothing had happened. I felt pleased that I might now make better drawings than before; and, ere a period not exceeding three years had elapsed, my portfolio was again filled."

The accidental destruction of Sir Isaac Newton's papers, by his little dog 'Diamond' upsetting a lighted taper upon his desk, by which the elaborate calculations of many years were in a moment destroyed, is a well-known anecdote, and need not be repeated: it is said that the loss caused the philosopher such profound grief that it seriously injured his health, and impaired his understanding. An accident of a somewhat similar kind happened to the MS. of Mr. Carlyle's first volume of his 'French Revolution.' He had lent the MS. to a literary neighbour to peruse. By some mischance, it had been left lying on the parlour floor, and become forgotten. Weeks ran on, and the historian sent for his work, the printers being loud for "copy." Inquiries were made, and it was found that the maid-of-all-work, finding what she conceived to be a bundle of waste paper on the floor, had used it to light the kitchen and parlour fires with! Such was the answer returned to Mr. Carlyle; and his feelings may be imagined. There was, however, no help for him but to set resolutely to work to re-write the book; and he turned to and did it. He had no draft, and was compelled to rake up from his memory facts, ideas, and expressions, which had been long since dismissed. The composition of the book in the first instance had been a work of pleasure; the re-writing of it a second time was one of pain and anguish almost beyond belief. That he persevered and finished the volume under such circumstances, affords an instance of determination of purpose which has seldom been surpassed.

HELP AND OPPORTUNITIES—SCIENTIFIC PURSUITS

ACCIDENT does very little towards the production of any great result in life. Though sometimes what is called "a happy hit" may be made by a bold venture, the common highway of steady industry and application is the only safe road to travel. It is said of the landscape painter Wilson, that when he had nearly finished a picture in a tame, correct manner, he would step back from it, his pencil fixed at the end of a long stick, and after gazing earnestly on the work, he would suddenly walk up and by a few bold touches give a brilliant finish to the painting. But it will not do for every one who would produce an effect, to throw his brush at the canvas in the hope of producing a picture. The capability of putting in these last vital touches is acquired only by the labour of a life; and the probability is, that the artist who has not carefully trained himself beforehand, in attempting to produce a brilliant effect at a dash, will only produce a blotch.

Sedulous attention and painstaking industry always mark the true worker. The greatest men are not those who "despise the day of small things," but those who improve them the most carefully. Michael Angelo was one day explaining to a visitor at his studio, what he had been doing at a statue since his previous visit. "I have retouched this part—polished that—softened this feature—brought out that muscle—given some expression to this lip, and more energy to that limb." "But these are trifles," remarked the visitor. "It may be so," replied the sculptor, "but recollect that trifles make perfection, and perfection is no trifle." So it was said of Nicholas Poussin, the painter, that the rule of his conduct was, that "whatever was worth doing at all was worth doing well;" and when asked, late in life, by his friend Vigneul de Marville, by what means he had gained so high a reputation among the painters of Italy, Poussin emphatically answered, "Because I have neglected nothing."

Although there are discoveries which are said to have been made by accident, if carefully inquired into, it will be found that there has really been very little that was accidental about them. For the most part, these so-called accidents have only been opportunities, carefully improved by genius. The fall of the apple at Newton's feet has often been quoted in proof of the accidental character of some discoveries. But Newton's whole mind had already been devoted for years to the laborious and patient investigation of the subject of gravitation; and the circumstance of the apple falling before his eyes was suddenly apprehended only as genius could apprehend it, and served to flash upon him the brilliant discovery then opening to his sight. In like manner, the brilliantly-coloured soap-bubbles blown from a common tobacco pipe—though "trifles light as air" in most eyes—suggested to Dr. Young his beautiful theory of "interferences," and led to his discovery relating to the diffraction of light. Although great men are popularly supposed only to deal with great things, men such as Newton and Young were ready to detect the significance of the most familiar and simple facts; their greatness consisting mainly in their wise interpretation of them.

ENERGY AND COURAGE

THERE is a famous speech recorded of an old Norseman, thoroughly characteristic of the Teuton. "I believe neither in idols nor demons," said he, "I put my sole trust in my own strength of body and soul." The ancient crest of a pickaxe with the motto of "Either I will find a way or make one," was an expression of the same sturdy independence which to this day distinguishes the descendants of the Northmen. Indeed nothing could be more characteristic of the Scandinavian mythology, than that it had a god with a hammer. A man's character is seen in small matters; and from even so slight a test as the mode in which a man wields a hammer, his energy may in some measure be inferred. Thus an eminent Frenchman hit off in a single phrase the characteristic quality of the inhabitants of a particular district, in which a friend of his proposed to settle and buy land. "Beware," said he, "of making a purchase there; I know the men of that department; the pupils who come from it to our veterinary school at Paris *do nor strike hard upon the anvil*; they want energy; and you will not get a satisfactory return on any capital you may invest there." A fine and just appreciation of character, indicating the thoughtful observer; and strikingly illustrative of the fact that it is the energy of the individual men that gives strength to a State, and confers a value even upon the very soil which they cultivate. As the French proverb has it: "Tant vaut l'homme, tant vaut sa terre."

The cultivation of this quality is of the greatest importance; resolute determination in the pursuit of worthy objects being the foundation of all true greatness of character. Energy enables a man to force his way through irksome drudgery and dry details, and carries him onward and upward in every station in life. It accomplishes more than genius, with not one-half the disappointment and peril. It is not eminent talent that is required to ensure success in any pursuit, so much as purpose,—not merely the power to achieve, but the will to labour energetically and perseveringly. Hence energy of will may be defined to be the very central power of character in a man—in a word, it is the Man himself. It gives impulse to his every action, and soul to every effort. True hope is based on it,—and it is hope that gives the real perfume to life. There is a fine heraldic motto on a broken helmet in Battle Abbey, "L'espoir est ma force," which might be the motto of every man's life. "Woe unto him that is fainthearted," says the son of Sirach. There is, indeed, no blessing equal to the possession of a stout heart. Even if a man fail in his efforts, it will be a satisfaction to him to enjoy the consciousness of having done his best. In humble life nothing can be more cheering and beautiful than to see a man combating suffering by patience, triumphing in his integrity, and who, when his feet are bleeding and his limbs failing him, still walks upon his courage.

Mere wishes and desires but engender a sort of green sickness in young minds, unless they are promptly embodied in act and deed. It will not avail merely to wait as so many do, "until Blucher comes up," but they must struggle on and persevere in the mean time, as Wellington did. The good purpose once formed must be carried out with alacrity and without swerving. In most conditions of life, drudgery and toil are to be cheerfully endured as the best and most wholesome discipline. "In life," said Ary Scheffer, "nothing bears fruit except by labour of mind or body. To strive and still strive—such is life; and in this respect mine is fulfilled; but I dare to say, with just pride, that nothing has ever shaken my courage. With a strong soul, and a noble aim, one can do what one wills, morally speaking."

SELF-CULTURE—FACILITIES AND DIFFICULTIES

THE best part of every man's education," said Sir Walter Scott, "is that which he gives to himself." The late Sir Benjamin Brodie delighted to remember this saying, and he used to congratulate himself on the fact that professionally he was self-taught. But this is necessarily the case with all men who have acquired distinction in letters, science, or art. The education received at school or college is but a beginning, and is valuable mainly inasmuch as it trains the mind and habituates it to continuous application and study. That which is put into us by others is always far less ours than that which we acquire by our own diligent and persevering effort. Knowledge conquered by labour becomes a possession—a property entirely our own. A greater vividness and permanency of impression is secured; and facts thus acquired become registered in the mind in a way that mere imparted information can never effect. This kind of self-culture also calls forth power and cultivates strength. The solution of one problem helps the mastery of another; and thus knowledge is carried into faculty. Our own active effort is the essential thing; and no facilities, no books, no teachers, no amount of lessons learnt by rote will enable us to dispense with it.

The best teachers have been the readiest to recognize the importance of self-culture, and of stimulating the student to acquire knowledge by the active exercise of his own faculties. They have relied more upon *training* than upon telling, and sought to make their pupils themselves active parties to the work in which they were engaged; thus making teaching something far higher than the mere passive reception of the scraps and details of knowledge.

This was the spirit in which the great Dr. Arnold worked; he strove to teach his pupils to rely upon themselves, and develop their powers by their own active efforts, himself merely guiding, directing, stimulating, and encouraging them. "I would far rather," he said, "send a boy to Van Diemen's Land, where he must work for his bread, than send him to Oxford to live in luxury, without any desire in his mind to avail himself of his advantages." "If there be one thing on earth," he observed on another occasion, "which is truly admirable, it is to see God's wisdom blessing an inferiority of natural powers, when they have been honestly, truly, and zealously cultivated." Speaking of a pupil of this character, he said, "I would stand to that man hat in hand." Once at Laleham, when teaching a rather dull boy, Arnold spoke somewhat sharply to him, on which the pupil looked up in his face and said, "Why do you speak angrily, sir? *indeed*, I am doing the best I can." Years afterwards, Arnold used to tell the story to his children, and added, "I never felt so much in my life—that look and that speech I have never forgotten."

Self-discipline and self-control are the beginnings of practical wisdom; and these must have their root in self-respect. Hope springs from it—hope, which is the companion of power, and the mother of success; for whoso hopes strongly has within him the gift of miracles. The humblest may say, "To respect myself, to develop myself—

this is my true duty in life. An integral and responsible part of the great system of society, I owe it to society and to its Author not to degrade or destroy either my body, mind, or instincts. On the contrary, I am bound to the best of my power to give to those parts of my constitution the highest degree of perfection possible. I am not only to suppress the evil, but to evoke the good elements in my nature. And as I respect myself, so am I equally bound to respect others, as they on their part are bound to respect me." Hence mutual respect, justice, and order, of which law becomes the written record and guarantee.

Self-respect is the noblest garment with which a man may clothe himself—the most elevating feeling with which the mind can be inspired. One of Pythagoras's wisest maxims, in his 'Golden Verses,' is that with which he enjoins the pupil to "reverence himself." Borne up by this high idea, he will not defile his body by sensuality, nor his mind by servile thoughts. This sentiment, carried into daily life, will be found at the root of all the virtues—cleanliness, sobriety, chastity, morality, and religion. "The pious and just honouring of ourselves," said Milton, "may be thought the radical moisture and fountain-head from whence every laudable and worthy enterprise issues forth." To think meanly of one's self, is to sink in one's own estimation as well as in the estimation of others. And as the thoughts are, so will the acts be. Man cannot aspire if he look down; if he will rise, he must look up. The very humblest may be sustained by the proper indulgence of this feeling. Poverty itself may be lifted and lighted up by self-respect; and it is truly a noble sight to see a poor man hold himself upright amidst his temptations, and refuse to demean himself by low actions.

One way in which self-culture may be degraded is by regarding it too exclusively as a means of "getting on." Viewed in this light, it is unquestionable that education is one of the best investments of time and labour. In any line of life, intelligence will enable a man to adapt himself more readily to circumstances, suggest improved methods of working, and render him more apt, skilled and effective in all respects. He who works with his head as well as his hands, will come to look at his business with a clearer eye; and he will become conscious of increasing power— perhaps the most cheering consciousness the human mind can cherish. The power of self-help will gradually grow; and in proportion to a man's self-respect, will he be armed against the temptation of low indulgences. Society and its action will be regarded with quite a new interest, his sympathies will widen and enlarge, and he will thus be attracted to work for others as well as for himself.

CHARACTER—THE TRUE GENTLEMAN

THE crown and glory of life is Character. It is the noblest possession of a man, constituting a rank in itself, and an estate in the general goodwill; dignifying every station, and exalting every position in society. It exercises a greater power than wealth, and secures all the honour without the jealousies of fame. It carries with it an influence which always tells; for it is the result of proved honour, rectitude, and consistency—qualities which, perhaps more than any other, command the general confidence and respect of mankind.

Character is human nature in its best form. It is moral order embodied in the individual. Men of character are not only the conscience of society, but in every well-governed State they are its best motive power; for it is moral qualities in the main which rule the world. Even in war, Napoleon said the moral is to the physical as ten to one. The strength, the industry, and the civilisation of nations—all depend upon individual character; and the very foundations of civil security rest upon it. Laws and institutions are but its outgrowth. In the just balance of nature, individuals, nations, and races, will obtain just so much as they deserve, and no more. And as effect finds its cause, so surely does quality of character amongst a people produce its befitting results.

Though a man have comparatively little culture, slender abilities, and but small wealth, yet, if his character be of sterling worth, he will always command an influence, whether it be in the workshop, the counting-house, the mart, or the senate. Canning wisely wrote in 1801, "My road must be through Character to power; I will try no other course; and I am sanguine enough to believe that this course, though not perhaps the quickest, is the surest." You may admire men of intellect; but something more is necessary before you will trust them. Hence Lord John Russell once observed in a sentence full of truth, "It is the nature of party in England to ask the assistance of men of genius, but to follow the guidance of men of character." This was strikingly illustrated in the career of the late Francis Horner—a man of whom Sydney Smith said that the Ten Commandments were stamped upon his countenance. "The valuable and peculiar light," says Lord Cockburn, "in which his history is calculated to inspire every right-minded youth, is this. He died at the age of thirty-eight; possessed of greater public influence than any other private man; and admired, beloved, trusted, and deplored by all, except the heartless or the base. No greater homage was ever paid in Parliament to any deceased member. Now let every young man ask—how was this attained? By rank? He was the son of an Edinburgh merchant. By wealth? Neither he, nor any of his relations, ever had a superfluous sixpence. By office? He held but one, and only for a few years, of no influence, and with very little pay. By talents? His were not splendid, and he had no genius. Cautious and slow, his only ambition was to be right. By eloquence? He spoke in calm, good taste, without any of the oratory that either terrifies or seduces. By any fascination of manner? His was only correct and agreeable. By what, then, was it? Merely by sense, industry, good principles, and a good heart—qualities which no well-constituted mind need ever despair of attaining. It was the force of his character that raised him; and this character not impressed upon him by nature, but formed, out of no peculiarly fine elements, by himself. There were many in the House of Commons of far greater ability and eloquence. But no one surpassed him in the combination of an adequate portion of these with moral worth. Horner was born to show what moderate powers, unaided by anything whatever except culture and goodness, may achieve, even when these powers are displayed amidst the competition and jealousy of public life."

Gentleness is indeed the best test of gentlemanliness. A consideration for the feelings of others, for his inferiors and dependants as well as his equals, and respect for their self-respect, will pervade the true gentleman's whole conduct. He will rather himself suffer a small injury, than by an uncharitable construction of another's behaviour, incur the risk of committing a great wrong. He will be forbearant of the weaknesses, the failings, and the errors, of those whose advantages in life have not been equal to his own. He will be merciful even to his beast. He will not boast of his wealth, or his strength, or his gifts. He will not be puffed up by success, or unduly depressed by failure. He will not obtrude his views on others, but speak his mind freely when occasion calls for it. He will not confer favours with a patronizing air.

- We often discover what will do, by finding out what will not do; and probably he who never made a mistake, never made a discovery.
- Enthusiasm is the sustaining power of all great action.
- The reason why so little is done, is generally because so little is attempted. So attempt more.
- Hope is the companion of power, and mother of success; for who so hopes strongly has within him the gift of miracles.
- Lost wealth may be replaced by industry, lost knowledge by study, lost health by temperance or medicine, but lost time is gone forever.

TEN

How to Connect with Your 'Inner Self' in Uncertain Times

Henry David Thoreau answers from *Walden*

While Thoreau lived at Walden (1845–1847), he wrote journal entries and prepared lyceum lectures on his experiment in living at the pond. By 1847, he had begun to set his first draft of Walden *down on paper. After leaving Walden, he expanded and reworked his material repeatedly until the spring of 1854, producing a total of eight versions of the book.*

Although Thoreau actually lived at Walden for two years, Walden *is a narrative of his life at the pond compressed into the cycle of a single year, from spring to spring.*

〰

We must learn to reawaken and keep ourselves awake, not by mechanical aids, but by an infinite expectation of the dawn, which does not forsake us in our soundest sleep. I know of no more encouraging fact than the unquestionable ability of man to elevate his life by a conscious endeavor. It is something to be able to paint a particular picture, or to carve a statue, and so to make a few objects beautiful; but it is far more glorious to carve and paint the very atmosphere and medium through which we look, which morally we can do. To affect the quality of the day, that is the highest of arts. Every man is tasked to make his life, even in its details, worthy of the contemplation of his most elevated and critical hour. If we refused, or rather used up, such paltry information as we get, the oracles would distinctly inform us how this might be done.

I went to the woods because I wished to live deliberately, to front only the essential facts of life, and see if I could not learn what it had to teach, and not, when I came to die, discover that I had not lived. I did not wish to live what was not life, living is so dear; nor did I wish to practise resignation, unless it was quite necessary. I wanted to live deep and suck out all the marrow of life, to live so sturdily and Spartan-like as to put to rout all that was not life, to cut a broad swath and shave close, to drive life into a corner, and reduce it to its lowest terms, and, if it proved to be mean, why then to get the whole and genuine meanness of it, and publish its meanness to the world; or if it were sublime, to know it by experience, and be able to give a true account of it in my next excursion. For most men, it appears to me, are in a strange uncertainty about it, whether it is of the devil or of God, and have somewhat hastily concluded that it is the chief end of man here to "glorify God and enjoy him forever."

Still we live meanly, like ants; though the fable tells us that we were long ago changed into men; like pygmies we fight with cranes; it is error upon error, and clout upon clout, and our best virtue has for its occasion a superfluous and evitable wretchedness. Our life is frittered away by detail. An honest man has hardly need to count more than his ten fingers, or in extreme cases he may add his ten toes, and lump the rest. Simplicity, simplicity, simplicity! I say, let your affairs be as two or three, and not a hundred or a thousand; instead of a million count half a dozen, and keep your accounts on your thumb nail. In the midst of this chopping sea of civilized life, such are the clouds and storms and quicksands and thousand-and-one items to be allowed for, that a man has to live, if he would not founder and go to the bottom and not make his port at all, by dead reckoning, and he must be a great calculator indeed who succeeds. Simplify, simplify. Instead of three meals a day, if it be necessary eat but one; instead of a hundred dishes, five; and reduce other things in proportion. Our life is like a German Confederacy, made up of petty states, with its boundary forever fluctuating, so that even a German cannot tell you how it is bounded at any moment. The nation itself, with all its so called internal improvements, which, by the way are all external and superficial, is just such an unwieldy and overgrown establishment, cluttered with furniture and tripped up by its own traps, ruined by luxury and heedless expense, by want of calculation and a worthy aim, as the million households in the land; and the only cure for it as for them is in a rigid economy, a stern and more than Spartan simplicity of life and elevation of purpose. It lives too fast. Men think that it is essential that the Nation have commerce, and export ice, and talk through a telegraph, and ride thirty miles an hour, without a doubt, whether they do or not; but whether we should live like baboons or like men, is a little uncertain. If we do not get out sleepers, and forge rails, and devote days and nights to the work, but go to tinkering upon our lives to improve them, who will build railroads? And if railroads are not built, how shall we get to heaven in season? But if we stay at home and mind our business, who will want railroads? We do not ride on the railroad; it rides upon us. Did you ever think what those sleepers are that underlie the railroad? Each one is a man, an Irish-man, or a Yankee man. The rails are laid on them, and they are covered with sand, and the cars run smoothly over them. They are sound sleepers, I assure you. And every few years a new lot is laid down and run over; so that, if some have the pleasure of riding on a rail, others have the misfortune to be ridden upon. And when they run over a man that is walking in his sleep, a supernumerary sleeper in the wrong position, and wake him up, they suddenly stop the cars, and make a hue and cry about it, as if this were an exception. I am glad to know that it takes a gang of men for every five miles to keep the sleepers down and level in their beds as it is, for this is a sign that they may sometime get up again.

Why should we live with such hurry and waste of life? We are determined to be starved before we are hungry. Men say that a stitch in time saves nine, and so they take a thousand stitches to-day to save nine to-morrow. As for work, we haven't any of any consequence. We have the Saint Vitus' dance, and cannot possibly keep our heads still. If I should only give a few pulls at the parish bell-rope, as for a fire, that is, without setting the bell, there is hardly a man on his farm in the outskirts of Concord, notwithstanding that press of engagements which was his excuse so many times this morning, nor a boy, nor a woman, I might almost say, but would forsake all and follow that sound, not mainly to save property from the flames, but, if we will confess the truth, much more to see it burn, since burn it must, and we, be it known, did not set it on fire,—or to see it put out, and have a hand in it, if that is done as handsomely; yes, even if it were the parish church itself. Hardly a man takes a half hour's nap after dinner, but when he wakes he holds up his head and asks, "What's the news?" as if the rest of mankind had stood his sentinels. Some give directions to be waked every half hour, doubtless for no other purpose; and then, to pay for it, they tell what they have dreamed. After a night's sleep the news is as indispensable as the breakfast. "Pray tell me any thing new that has happened to a man any where on this globe,"—and he reads it over his coffee and rolls, that a man has had his eyes gouged out this morning on the Wachito River; never dreaming the while that he lives in the dark unfathomed mammoth cave of this world, and has but the rudiment of an eye himself.

Shams and delusions are esteemed for soundest truths, while reality is fabulous. If men would steadily observe realities only, and not allow themselves to be deluded, life, to compare it with such things as we know, would be like a fairy tale and the Arabian Nights' Entertainments. If we respected only what is inevitable and has a right to be, music and poetry would resound along the streets. When we are unhurried and wise, we perceive that only great and worthy things have any permanent and absolute existence— that petty fears and petty pleasures are but the shadow of the reality. This is always exhilarating and sublime. By closing the eyes and slumbering, and consenting to be deceived by shows, men establish and confirm their daily life of routine and habit everywhere, which still is built on purely illusory foundations. Children, who play life, discern its true law and relations more clearly than men, who fail to live it worthily, but who think that they are wiser by experience, that is, by failure. I have read in a Hindoo book, that "there was a king's son, who, being expelled in infancy from his native city, was brought up by a forester, and, growing up to maturity in that state, imagined himself to belong to the barbarous race with which he lived. One of his father's ministers having discovered him, revealed to him what he was, and the misconception of his character was removed, and he knew himself to be a prince. So soul," continues the Hindoo philosopher, "from the circumstances in which it is placed, mistakes its own character, until the truth is revealed to it by some holy teacher, and then it knows itself to be Brahme." I perceive that we inhabitants of New England live this mean life that we do because our vision does not penetrate the surface of things. We think that that is which appears to be. If a man should walk through this town and see only the reality, where, think you, would the "Mill-dam" go to? If he should give us an account of the realities he beheld there, we should not recognize the place in his description. Look at a meeting-house, or a court-house, or a jail, or a shop, or a dwelling-house, and say what that thing really is before a true gaze, and they would all go to pieces in your account of them. Men esteem truth remote, in the outskirts of the system, behind the farthest star, before Adam and after the last man. In eternity there is indeed something true and sublime. But all these times and places and occasions are now and here. God himself culminates in the present moment, and will never be more divine in the lapse of all the ages. And we are enabled to apprehend at all what is sublime and noble only by the perpetual instilling and drenching of the reality that surrounds us. The universe constantly and obediently answers to our conceptions; whether we travel fast or slow, the track is laid for us. Let us spend our lives in conceiving then. The poet or the artist never yet had so fair and noble a design but some of his posterity at least could accomplish it.

Let us spend one day as deliberately as Nature, and not be thrown off the track by every nutshell and mosquito's wing that falls on the rails. Let us rise early and fast, or break fast, gently and without perturbation; let company come and let company go, let the bells ring and the children cry—determined to make a day of it. Why should we knock under and go with the stream? Let us not be upset and overwhelmed in that terrible rapid and whirlpool called a dinner, situated in the meridian shallows. Weather this danger and you are safe, for the rest of the way is down hill. With unrelaxed nerves, with morning vigor, sail by it, looking another way, tied to the mast like Ulysses. If the engine whistles, let it whistle till it is hoarse for its pains. If the bell rings, why should we run? We will consider what kind of music they are like. Let us settle ourselves, and work and wedge our feet downward through the mud and slush of opinion, and prejudice, and tradition, and delusion, and appearance, that alluvion which covers the globe, through Paris and London, through New York and Boston and Concord, through church and state, through poetry and philosophy and religion, till we come to a hard bottom and rocks in place, which we can call reality, and say, This is, and no mistake; and then begin, having a point d'appui, below freshet and frost and fire, a place where you might found a wall or a state, or set a lamp-post safely, or perhaps a gauge, not a Nilometer, but a Realometer, that future ages might know how deep a freshet of shams and appearances had gathered from time to time. If you stand right fronting and face to face to a fact, you will see the sun glimmer on both its surfaces, as if it were a cimeter, and feel its sweet edge dividing you through the heart and marrow, and so you will happily conclude your mortal career. Be it life or death, we crave only reality. If we are really dying, let us hear the rattle in our throats and feel cold in the extremities; if we are alive, let us go about our business.

IN THE END

Rather than love, than money, than fame, give me truth. I sat at a table where were rich food and wine in abundance, and obsequious attendance, but sincerity and truth were not; and I went away hungry from the inhospitable board. The hospitality was as cold as the ices. I thought that there was no need of ice to freeze them. They talked to me of the age of the wine and the fame of the vintage; but I thought of an older, a newer, and purer wine, of a more glorious vintage, which they had not got, and could not buy. The style, the house and grounds and "entertainment" pass for nothing with me. I called on the king, but he made me wait in his hall, and conducted like a man incapacitated for hospitality. There was a man in my neighborhood who lived in a hollow tree. His manners were truly regal. I should have done better had I called on him.

How long shall we sit in our porticoes practicing idle and musty virtues, which any work would make impertinent? As if one were to begin the day with long-suffering, and hire a man to hoe his potatoes; and in the afternoon go forth to practise Christian meekness and charity with goodness aforethought! Consider the China pride and stagnant self-complacency of mankind. This generation inclines a little to congratulate itself on being the last of an illustrious line; and in Boston and London and Paris and Rome, thinking of its long descent, it speaks of its progress in art and science and literature with satisfaction. There are the Records of the Philosophical Societies, and the public Eulogies of Great Men! It is the good Adam contemplating his own virtue. "Yes, we have done great deeds, and sung divine songs, which shall never die,"—that is, as long as we can remember them. The learned societies and great men of Assyria,—where are they? What youthful philosophers and experimentalists we are! There is not one of my readers who has yet lived a whole human life. These may be but the spring months in the life of the race. If we have had the seven-years' itch, we have not seen the seventeen-year locust yet in Concord. We are acquainted with a mere pellicle of the globe on which we live. Most have not delved six feet beneath the surface, nor leaped as many above it. We know not where we are. Beside, we are sound asleep nearly half our time. Yet we esteem ourselves wise, and have an established order on the surface. Truly, we are deep thinkers, we are ambitious spirits! As I stand over the insect crawling amid the pine needles on the forest floor, and endeavoring to conceal itself from my sight, and ask myself why it will cherish those humble thoughts, and hide its head from me who might, perhaps, be its benefactor, and impart to its race some cheering information, I am reminded of the greater Benefactor and Intelligence that stands over me the human insect.

There is an incessant influx of novelty into the world, and yet we tolerate incredible dulness. I need only suggest what kind of sermons are still listened to in the most enlightened countries. There are such words as joy and sorrow, but they are only the burden of a psalm, sung with a nasal twang, while we believe in the ordinary and mean. We think that we can change our clothes only. It is said that the British Empire is very large and respectable, and that the United States are a first-rate power. We do not believe that a tide rises and falls behind every man which can float the British Empire like a chip, if he should ever harbor it in his mind. Who knows what sort of seventeen-year locust will next come out of the ground? The government of the world I live in was not framed, like that of Britain, in after-dinner conversations over the wine.

The life in us is like the water in the river. It may rise this year higher than man has ever known it, and flood the parched uplands; even this may be the eventful year, which will drown out all our muskrats. It was not always dry land where we dwell. I see far inland the banks which the stream anciently washed, before science began to record its freshets. Every one has heard the story which has gone the rounds of New England, of a strong and beautiful bug which came out of the dry leaf of an old table of apple-tree wood, which had stood in a farmer's kitchen for sixty years, first in Connecticut, and afterward in Massachusetts—from an egg deposited in the living tree many years earlier still, as appeared by counting the annual layers beyond it; which was heard gnawing out for several weeks, hatched perchance by the heat of an urn. Who does not feel his faith in a resurrection and immortality strengthened by hearing of this? Who knows what beautiful and winged life, whose egg has been buried for ages under many concentric layers of woodenness in the dead dry life of society, deposited at first in the alburnum of the green and living tree, which has been gradually converted into the semblance of its well-seasoned tomb,—heard perchance gnawing out now for years by the astonished family of man, as they sat round the festive board,—may unexpectedly come forth from amidst society's most trivial and handselled furniture, to enjoy its perfect summer life at last!

- Mad pursuit of wealth and pleasure has made men desperate and isolated.
- One should go confidently in the direction of his dreams.
- The question is not what you look at, but what you see.
- If we will be quiet and ready enough, we shall find compensation in every disappointment.
- Don't look at things, see them.